Azure Tides

David A Trotter

DEDICATION

This book is dedicated to my three best friends. Few in life get the opportunity to gain a single friend for life. I have been blessed with three. So, this one is for the boys! Thank you, Cameron, Dalton, and Taylor. Life would be a lot duller without you three in it. Each of you bring your own unique personalities and 'flavor' to the friendship. It was your friendship that inspired Quickfingers and Lightfoot's, as you will see depicted throughout this s

@DAT PUBLISHING, LLC

ISBN: 978-1-7378655-4-4

CONTENTS

ACKNOWLEDGMENTS

This book would not have happened without the support of the following individuals:

First, my wife, Heather Trotter, who supports me and my writing in a way that can only be described as selfless and enduring. I love you.

Second, Aaron Moschner, Robert Zangari, Ellie Drees, and Henry Kramer. Each of you hold unique place in the world of Ethrea and the creation of Azure Tides.

Third, to my family, with a special shoutout to my sister, Laura Deason! Thank you all for being awesome.

Finally, each and everyone of you who pledged your support via Kickstarter. Without your pledge, I never would have completed this work. Thank you to the following:

Amazing Sauce, The Fantastic Robert Zangari, Tyler DeJong, Abdul Hadi Sid Ahmed, Richard Black, Richard Fierce, Caleb Slama, Josh Samples, Kyle G Wilkinson, Ellie Drees, Cameron Sjo, Gerald P. McDaniel, Rob Steinberger, Steven M Tyler, Andrew Claydon, Austin Hoffey, N. Scott Pearson, C. Wilson, Rachael E Garrett, Margo Bond Collins, Alicia P., Steven A. Guglich, Algie Lane III, TJ McDonald, Paul Smith, Dan Kenner, Cami Murdock Jensen, Brandon Bender, Chris Session, Andrew Franklin, Sydney Lewis, Engel Dreizehn, H Joseph, Cameron Cathcart, Caio Maida, Leslie Twitchell, Kyle J Cisco, Anil Kadam, NeonPixxius, Karen Bulgarelli, Robert K. Barbour , Quentin Foster, Lark Cunningham, Hana Correa, Miz Swift, Isidoro, Cesar, Leo Cortes, Kaladin son of Mason, Connor Barber, Ian Bannon, Brier Jones, Katherine Shipman, Ruthenia, Tectaru of Vana'diel, Master White Mage, Tamara Hart Heiner, Jeffrey M. Johnson, and many others who chose to remain anonymous.

THANK YOU!

Chapter 1: Upper Deck

Gulls squealed their high-pitch songs of dissonant bartering as they fought over crumbs and waste. Sprays of white-foam saltwater misted over the deck of the Pearl of Red Duchess as Seamus Pearson scrubbed on hands and knees, splotching his bare, bony back with cool reprieve. The sun hung high, the stifling heat mixing with the scent of fish and saltwater filled his nostrils with a nearly unbearable aroma, that and the lye used to scrub the endless panels of wood that made up the upper deck.

Three years upon the Pearl of Red Duchess and still Seamus scrubbed and scrubbed. True, he could have paid off his debt the prior year, but Seamus had a nasty habit. The same that had landed him his iron collar, and had given him his calloused hands and feet. He was a thief. And not a very good one at that. But, to his credit, he had nearly gotten away with his last score- had his 'best' mate had not sold him out for an apple, a bit of cheese, and two days of sleeping out of the enormous galleon's musty hold.

Blasted, curdled wad of spit! Fumed Seamus fumed as he imagined Henri 'Lightfoot' Sjo eating cheese right about now, relaxed and comfortable. *I hope he chokes!*

Seamus didn't actually hope the lad choked. Not really. In all honesty, he would have done the same had he thought about it quicker. Seamus had always prided himself in being the quick-thinker of the two, but the proof was in the work'n, and Lightfoot wasn't scrub'n the decks today, now was he?

"Oye!" Called out the barrel-chested Master O'Decks. "Ya best be scrub'n harder'n that or you'll be here past nightfall, ya will!"

"Aye, sir," Seamus groaned as he tugged at the irons around his scrawny, pale neck. Well, pale as could be for spending day after day in the sun. Seamus was not a Galacian by birth, but a Transplant as they'd call'em.

"It do be a shame ya got stuck with them there irons again there, laddie," the fat Master laughed as he stroked his salt and pepper mustache with sausage-like fingers, each covered with blackened-iron rings. His bare, sun-tanned forearms were wrapped with corded muscles and decorated with black tattoos.

"Don't sound too worked up, Charlie. You'd be going soft if y'er did."

"Boy, best be calling me by my title if ya want that their choker off ya tonight. Now be a good lad and bow real nice and scrub a little hard now," Master Charlie chuckled without any malice at all in his voice, just a grumble of easy amusement.

"Oye, I'll do that I will! Master, sir!" Seamus said as he swung his hand up to his brow in a sardonic salute that flung suds and water all over the wrinkled shirt of that fat Master O'Decks.

"Ha!" bellowed Master Charlie, wiping a laughing tear from his watery grey eye. "By the god's own hand, y'er the son I never had, that y'er are. It's a right shame I'll have to have you taken down a notch with the rod tonight instead of taking off them irons now."

"I'm sure you're truly torn up about it," Seamus grimaced as he plopped back onto his hands and began scrubbing with a huff. "Right torn up indeed."

"I'll tell y'er what, laddie," the man said as looked over the immense deck. Smiling up at the three towering beams that made up the forward masts, from which majestic white sales caught the gentle breeze and puffed outwards, and then back to the grainy wood upon which they stood. "You go and scrub these real fine like and I'll remove that collar and won't be taking the rod to y'er tonight. How's that sound?"

"Aye, I can do that," Seamus said, trying not to reveal the relief in his voice. He had always had a sharp mouth and a sense for the wrong thing, but he knew a good thing when offered, and he would take any bit of ease he could.

"Good then!" Master Charlie barked loudly, straightening up to a towering height. His knee-high leather boots did not reflect Seamus's gaunt face as they had done when they were calling to port. And the white britches, with bold blue stripes running through them, were not lined up as smartly as they would be on inspection day. But that was to be expected when one was at sea. Formalities be damned. "Clean this up and report to my chambers at sun fall. Dismissed!"

Seamus laughed as the fat man stomped proudly away. He hadn't smelt like booze in the slightest, which was quite the rarity for being out at sea for as long as they had been. As a matter of fact, Seamus mused, not many had smelled like the liquor this whole trip, save Scurvy Mau and Frazzle-Beard Ruyn. And those two always smelled of the bottle, regardless of time, company, or day.

What made this trip so important? Too many things off about it, there were. Firstly, Lightfoot wouldn't have doubled crossed Seamus 'Quickfingers' normally. He had been growing some bones that boy had been. Lightfoot hadn't always been the thieving kind, but hunger will do that to a lad, ain't no questions asked there. Not one. Secondly, Master Charlie was practically Seamus's own Pa by terms now. He wasn't like to be doling out stiff punishments like this, especially not talking about the rod and chains. No, something was off about this all in all. And the nail in the plank, it was that High Captain Atura'poha'alana herself had not but to say where they were sailing off too. Not a word. Not a notion of direction. By the sun and moon and the stars it could be worked out they were heading Westward. But to where? No one would seem to answer him.

Seamus looked out over the railing of the starboard quarter and gazed at the tiny specks that made up the Far Western Isles, slowly disappearing over the horizon. The gulls would soon vanish, being too far from land made the blasted white birds uncomfortable. And that was all for the better. Their ceaseless cries and endless droppings made Seamus's days a farsight worse than they should be. *But, if they were already passing the Western Isles, where in the name of the Great Goddess Gallae were they headed?*

Supper bells rang out low and long as the sun's rays turned the seas into an endless, shimmering, mirror of amber light. Seamus Quickfingers looked up in astonishment. It was surprising how slowly time moved when performing back-breaking, manual labor. It seemed like a hundred hours had passed in the time it had taken him to scrub the Upper Deck.

But the job was done, and technically before supper.

"It's a shame, Quickie," came a sly, girlish voice. "You don't live up to your name when you come to cleaning. What good is a man who cannot clean or be obedient?"

"Oye," Seamus retorted with an air of not-so-feigned frustration. "Snapdragon, that you there? Ain't you got a Mistress to be groveling beneath?"

"A good man learns to mind his tongue, Quickie," the girl snapped with an upturn of her nose in a snooty manner.

"Well thank the Golden Goddess then, I ain't no good man!"

"Hey! Mind the way you speak of the Holy Mother!" The playfulness had vanished from the young girl's voice, and her deep brown eyes hardened noticeably on Seamus.

"I ain't an acolyte, princess," Seamus snarled with noticeable frustration. "I can say what I want, when I want, where I want. Ain't no higher power I answer to but me."

"And here I was thinking I was the High Captain of this ship," came another, far more regal voice, a far more mature and commanding female voice. "Or do I mistake myself and my station?"

Seamus's heart could have fallen out of his mouth had his tongue not swelled to ten times its normal size. He fell face-first onto the deck, placing his hands over his head, palms turned upwards.

High Captain Atura'poha'alana, or as her crew called her, Captain Atura, was of native Galacian birth, and high birth at that. Only females in Galacain society could be High Captains, own land, or rule in government. The even Galacian King, Her Majesty Tunu'kuuna, Daughter of Tana'kuuna, was female. All rule, law, justice, and command were held by the fairer sex. For they were the Daughters of Dragons, formed in the belly of the Old Ones centuries past, the first of whom was Gallae, High Lady of the Ellitheor, whose name is borne by the Isles themselves.

"I did not think so," Captain Atura smirked as she placed her hands on her hips and stared down at Seamus.

Seamus looked up at the High Captain, and despite his utter fear and deepening embarrassment, his breath still caught as he looked at her. The women of the Isles were known for their beauty and ferocity, and the Goddess had given High Captain two shares of beauty and three of ferocity thought Seamus from his lowly station. She had curly black hair, pulled tight at the nape of her neck and a large, three-cornered Captain's hat of deep blue rested on her head. Her uniform was well fitted and imperial, though her womanly form was only amplified by this, a strange tradition the Galacain people seemed enthralled by. Women and men alike were known the world over for their provocative and brazen dress. And though, in uniform, fabric-covered nearly every inch of the Captain, the cloth was cut in such a manner that left little to the imagination. However, it was the dark markings across her chin and forehead that drew the most attention, tribal markings only befitting the highest of status.

"My Lady, your table awaits you," interrupted Snapdragon with a bow of her head, her own loose curls bobbing against her sun-kissed neck and tattooed upper back, which was bare save a wrap of fabric around her chest and three or four golden chains with large jade stones hanging from them, which jingled gently together.

"Do not let me catch you again, man-child, talking disrespectfully to another Wakatiti," Captain Atura snapped as the high heel of her boot clicked next to his head. "You are not on the Far Continent anymore. It is best you forget their foolish ways before you find yourself with irons about your boots out for a swim, savvy?"

"Yes, Ma'am! Er, Captain Mama!" Seamus blushed so deeply that there was not one patch of white skin that was not as red as his wiry hair.

"Good! Una'pahu, come." And with that sharp command, the High Captain turned on her heels, the tails of her long coat slapping Seamus in the reddened face, the hilt of curved saber only narrowly missing, and walked away.

Snapdragon did not look smug, but rather embarrassed as well.

"I'm sorry, Quickie, I should've told you she was behind me," she whispered into his ear, and then, if he was not already embarrassed enough, she kissed him on the cheek, in full view of the deck. And though no one stopped to look, for it was a Wakatiti's right to do as she pleases with whom she pleases, Seamus was not the most popular male on the Pearl of Red Duchess, and Una'pahu was of high birth on the Mother Isles.

Snapdragon's lips were soft, round, and moist. Despite the embarrassment, Seamus wished for more than a kiss on the cheek, but not on the open deck. Perhaps another night snuck out of his little hold beneath and up in her quarters? She did have a much softer bed, and her room did not smell like two hundred sailor's feet and unwashed buttocks. It was all he could do to not raise a hand and touch her bare stomach, to run his fingers on her smooth, soft, warm flesh. The tattoos of dragons, fish, waves and other marks that covered her skin only added to her allure. There weren't any women like this in Calun, that was certain, and perhaps this is why he had chosen to stay on The Peal another year.

"Don't get too excited, Msa'oo," she winked as she rose, extending a hand to help him up as if she could tell what he was thinking. But who wouldn't know what he was thinking? He was a seventeen-year-old, out at sea, with perhaps the most beautiful cultures of women, sitting across from one of their most blessed daughters. And he was without any way to work out his frustrations other than scrubbing a deck day in and day out. "And not tonight. I have training of my own to see too."

"As you wish, Wakatiti," Seamus said with a smirk

and a devilish laugh, though the disappointment was not well hidden.

"I said come, Una'pahu!" the High Captain shouted without turning her head. "Unless you wish to scrub the deck alongside this Mau?"

"Coming," Snapdragon answered hastily. She whirled away from Seamus as her tutor had, though it was not the tails of a Captain's coat that slapped him, but the wooden prayer beads tied into the strands of her opal and rust-colored huvu'huvu.

Seamus grunted and grabbed himself, the thin breeches not helping soften the myriad of connections with his manhood. All thoughts of a romantic night vanished swiftly from his mind as he dropped back to his knees in pain.

"Love hurts, don't it, lad?"

"For the love of the gods, is everyone about my business tonight?"

"You are my business, lad," chuckled Master Charlie.

"What did I do now?"

"It's supper time, and I do believe you are to be surviving me my meals tonight, as repayment for your scheme to try and swindle my favorite boots."

"Lightfoot was in on it too, and you know it! Why ain't he out here scrubbing and bringing you y'er food and drink?"

"Well that's a simple one, lad," the fat man boomed as he stroked his mustaches with glee. "He weren't dumb enough to try and go through with it. He wised up and just came forwards with it, instead of falling to the brunt of another one of your schemes. Ya know, you two have been about this same floating spit of wood for two years, and I do believe this was the first time he came forward before you did. The boy is wising up, he is. You best be learning from your own actions. I do think you thought that lad too clean about the edges. Ha! Karma do be that way, it does indeed!"

"Next time, I'll tie his feet up and put a red tower on his skull," Seamus grimaced.

"Ah, you'll not lay a finger on that boy," Charlie said, wiping away a tear from his eye.

"Oye, and why not?"

"Because, my boy, that there is the only real friend you do be having on this whole ship. Three hundred men and fifty-eighty women, not counting the cook and his staff or the pleasure seekers. Eight levels, including cargo space and three levels for guns, and ain't no other person taking a liking to you, besides Lightfoot, and perhaps me-self," Charlie answered with a dissipating chuckle.

"Naw," Seamus scoffed, though he knew the old man was probably right. "Snapdragon likes me well enough."

"Snapdragon?" Charlie said in a feigned voice of understanding, dripping with sarcasm. "That girl will cut your heart out and eat it in front of your own two eyes. Ain't no pretty woman that needs a man, is what my Pa always said. Best be believing that. Ain't not one! Besides, she is the daughter of Lord of Ships and

Commerce, the only title in all of Galacia that is held by a man. The only one, boy. If she won't eat your heart out, he'll for sure strap you to the end of a long gun and fire shot after shot till the black metal cooks y'er flesh to well done! Ha! You best be walking away from that mess as quick as your soap-white bare feet can take ya!"

"You're probably right," Seamus answered. But it was a long journey and he was miles away from the Lord of Ships and Commerce. And if Snapdragon wanted a warm body to lay next to and play games, who was he to deny her royal self? A thin smile drew across his white lips and he brushed his hair back out of his face. "Anyways, let's get you dinner."

"Oye, and then we can talk about taking off that collar," Master Charlie answered with a wink. "Looks mighty uncomfortable."

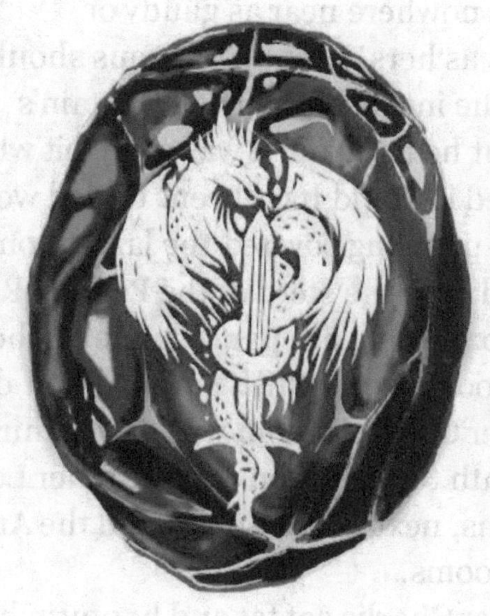

Chapter 2: Below Deck

The Pearl of Red Duchess was not a warship, not in truth, but it was one of the most heavily gunned ships in all of the Galacain's Armada. Frigates and other Man O'Wars made up the attacking force, but the Galleons of Galacia offered something even more powerful, luxurious travel. Kings and Queens, Tzars and Empresses, Lords and Ladies, and all other manner of royalty and the upper crust of society paid for passage aboard such fine vessels, and the Pearl of Red Duchess was the finest as they came.

The Master O'Decks had one of three personal cabins, other than the High Captain herself, and his own was nowhere near as gaudy or ostentatious as hers. In truth, Seamus should have never seen the inside of the High Captain's Quarters, but he had, and it was every bit what he had imagined it would have been. Gilded wood and painted paneling covered the large room, which rested atop the stern of the Pearl of Red Duchess. Dozens of glass panes made up the back wall of the room, from which embroidered drapes hung. Master Charlie's room was on the third level down, beneath Snapdragon and the other Leading Ladies' rooms, next to the Cook's and the Artillery Sergeant's rooms.

Master Charlie sat fat and happy in his oak armchair, his feet kicked up onto the small table and a pipe in his mouth, puffing long plumes of grey smoke. His cheeks were ruddy with drink, and his eyes ever so slightly droopy, as rum had oft affected him so. In a chair to his right was a thick lad with a broad back and heavy, albeit short beard. He had a dark, freckled face, black, curly hair, and eyes of dull hazel flecked with green. Bronze-rimmed spectacles sat on his stubby nose and the tip of a pink tongue poked out the side of his small mouth; he was clearly uncomfortable. Seamus sat to the left of the table, the iron collar no longer about his neck, in a dirty brown vest and with a sullen look on his face.

"Come on, boy," chuckled Master Charlie as he

blew out a big puff of smoke. "Eat your food and stop your sulking."

Lightfoot looked up, his piercing hazel eyes enlarged by the thick glass circles, directly at Seamus. His face bore a mixture of hurt and enthusiasm, though he was clearly trying hard to conceal the prior.

"You fat lump! I ought to-" Seamus started in, but Master Charlie raised a hand.

"Now, Henri, you got somethin to say too little Seamus here?"

"No," the boy called Lightfoot replied arrogantly. His voice was nasally, calculated, and altogether too proper. "I have nothing at all to say to him. He is just resentful that I bested him, that's all. If the tables were turned, he'd be laughing. I am merely enjoying a subtle victory."

"I ain't never seen anything like you two boys," sighed Master Charlie as he plopped his pipe down onto the old table.

"Get yourself a mirror and look at your ass, then you'd seen something like him," huffed Seamus.

"You're just jealous," snapped Henri.

"Jealous of what? It ain't your looks," Seamus leered. "Or your ability to look!"

"Oh, very original," sighed Henri with a roll of his eyes. "As if I've never heard a glasses joke before."

"Would a height joke have been better, you son of a dwarf's uncle?"

"Alright, alright. Enough is enough now boys. I can't have you snapping and each other like this, I have decks that needs scrubbing, and I sure as

Halfak's blazes ain't doing it. And I won't have you two killing each other while you're at it."

"But you said I'd get three days!" Henri groaned as he turned his glare to the fat Master.

"O? And you think I'll be giving you more than a day and a meal for helping plan the thievery of my own boots?" Master Charlie questioned, leaning his bulk onto the table and challenging Henri's stare.

The short lad shrunk back, a sulking grimace forming on his face. Seamus couldn't conceal the wry smile that was splitting his wind-chapped lips, nor did he try to.

"Don't think I didn't forget who actually took them," grunted Master Charlie as he laid a meaty hand on Seamus's thin, pale shoulder. "You got bones kid, the both of you do. And between ya both, you got half a brain, if you'd be willing to use it. But you won't get nowhere fast stab'n at each other's backs like this. Not where we're going. Not this time."

Seamus started up at that comment, eyes flashing with intrigue.

"You know where we're off too?"

"Of course I do, lad," Master Charlie chuckled, letting go of Seamus's shoulder and reaching for the nearly empty bottle of dark red rum. "But it's me job to know these things."

"Nobody on the crew seems to know," queried Lightfoot. "They've been oddly silent."

"About the King's business, we are," the fat

man stated between two deep gulps of rum, draining the bottle dry. "All y'er need to know about that, we be about her Royal Majesty's business. And you'r two ain't royal or got any business but scrub'n floors and dump'n pails. Leastwise unless y'er need to go scrape'n barnacles, do ya?"

"No sir!" Lightfoot said with an over-exaggerated surety.

"Pull your nose out, Lightfoot," Seamus said with a roll of his own eyes this time. True, the last time they had been sent over the edge of the Pearl, the waves had nearly knocked them into the sea. Seamus had never since trusted the dangling platform and had acquired a fear of dangling from high places without means of escape.

"I see no reason why I would want to provoke the man to send us out on those wretched scaffolds," sneered Lightfoot in reply, though the feigned venom and animosity between them had vanished as swiftly as the mention of where they could be off too.

"I know you're scared of heights, little Lightfoot," Seamus cackled. "But I'd do two over the edge if it meant getting away from the boots of this fat-"

A solid thud to the top of his head sent stars across Seamus's vision. Master Charlie was standing and looking rather displeased at the two of them, eyes swimming back and forth between them unsteadily.

"That was for the boots," he croaked. An open palm slapped Seamus across the face. The iron taste of blood filled his mouth, splitting his lip and causing his ears to ring. He then threw the empty rum bottle into

Henri's gut. The short lad let out an 'Oof!' as it struck him. "And that was for being a backstabbing little bastard!" Master Charlie then reached out with a deft speed that belied his drunkenness and caught them by the ears. "And if I hear either of you two causing any other commotion on this trip, I'll tan your hides and put you out to the fish! Do you understand me?"

"Yes sir!" Came the pain chorus from both squirming boys.

"Dismissed!" Master Charlie boomed and tossed both boys to the door.

The two fumbled to get upright awkwardly, helping and hindering the other as they scrambled to get out the too-small door frame that led into the Master O'Deck's cabin and out to the main level. Seamus' head was still spinning as he sprawled out onto the hallway's blue carpeted floor with a thud.

"You had to go and tell, didn't you?" he sneered as he picked himself up, two members of the mess staff stepped around him pretending that the teen didn't even exist.

"Tell him what? That you were planning to steal his boots and sell them to the chef for two silvers?" Lightfoot scoffed as he straightened his glasses. "I'm surprised you even got into his cabin before he thumped you. It was a foolish plan, Quickfingers, even for you."

"And yours to steal one of Snapdragon's huvu'huvu wasn't any better?" Seamus snapped, dusting off his threadbare vest.

"Oh," Henri laughed, and then lowered his voice and said. "That was solely because I knew you would go for it."

"But an iron collar and a firm slap ain't nothing to what we faced from her maids," Seamus whispered in reply, his wry smile returning slowly.

"It was downright deplorable what they asked," Henri chuckled. "And you didn't even get the skirt, did you Quickfingers?"

"Oh, you know," Seamus muttered, thankful his cheek was already red from the slap, as he ran his hand through his hair.

"You sly devil, you! You didn't tell me that you actually got your hands on it!"

"O," Seamus said with a wink. "I got my hands on it alright."

The humor drained from Lightfoot's face, replaced with a grimace of understanding. "By the Goddess Herself, you did not!"

"Listen, Lightfoot," Seamus said as he led his friend downstairs to the lower levels of the Pearl of Red Duchess. "When given an opportunity-"

"Only a fool refuses the moment," they both said in unison and Henri laid a hand on his friend's shoulder, and they laughed together as they made their way to the lowest level of the massive ship.

Two hammocks hung from the central beam, the feet of which tide to opposing holds, forming a 'V'. A circular rug, knit from rough cloth, lay on the floor between the two grey-cloth hammocks. A small table and two three-legged stools made up the only bit of furniture in their 'quarters'. Dozens of other set-ups as this lined the lower floor, where the lowest members of the ship's caste laid their heads to rest at night.

***

The morning came swiftly, the sun's golden rays glistened off the endless seas and lit the lower decks through small portholes covered with thick glass windows. The lower deck was a buzz of commotion as a hundred or so men moved about, giving their cots and hammocks up for those who had worked through the night. Seamus and Henri both rose and ready themselves for the day, pulling on their work garb and then folding their bedrolls away neatly. Despite the smell of men's odor and sea, the Pearl of Red Duchess was a tidy ship, kept proper and clean at all times and in all places.

Once on the Upper Deck, after a quick meal from the Mess, Henri and Seamus parted ways. Henri was a Captain's Aide, he was studying to become a navigator, and helped plot and plan where The Pearl would head too depending upon many things that were beyond Seamus's comprehension. But, his friend was happy doing what he did, so he tried not to bother him too much about it. What this did offer, was the ability to sneak away and spy about the ship, unperturbed.

Seamus, knowing that Master Charlie would not be about for at least another hour or so due to staff meetings, decided that today would be the day he would find some answers. It had bothered him, more deeply than he had let out, as to why The Pearl of Red Duchess was making this trip. This sentence reads really awkward. And more frustratingly tantalizing, was as to why it was being held to such secrecy.

The Council Room was a large room stationed below the Quarterdeck, on the third level of the ship, directly beneath the Captain's Chambers. It was a stately room, adorned with gilded walls, candelabras, velvet-covered chairs, and an oval rug of the deepest blue, whose entirety was stitched with scenes from Galacian lore. Fifteen persons sat in the room, each stationed in one of the high-back chairs, dressed in fine attire, both men and women alike. The Captain sat behind the only desk in the room, a stack of papers neatly rested to one side of her and a large map, topped with compass and sextant, was drawn out before her.

Seamus had snuck between the ventilation shaft, a small tunnel of wood that he could barely squeeze through, and watched through a small hole. He had bore that hole with a hand-crank months ago. He had even gone as far as pulling a matt into the tunnel, to provide him a soft space to lay and watch. Seamus had made this spot his personal attendance chamber to every important meeting this ship held and was the means by which he discovered many tightly held secrets. So, he lay still and listened.

"Now, see here," said a man whose hat was round and tall, and whose white mustaches were as prim as his Ordiatian accent, all filled with pride and cowardice. "We funded this expedition, you must hear what I have to say!"

"Lord Traegus," Captain Atura said in a level tone. "Despite your considerable donations to this expedition, and your namesake and close kinship to House Adelmo, you have little say in any of the operations of my ship. I do thank you for your patronage, Lord Traegus, but I will not have you patronizing me, my crew, or anyone else on this voyage."

Seamus had to bite his tongue to stifle a laugh. He quite enjoyed watching those of Tur'Mor and other paces on the Far Continent get levelly placed from his Captain. And, despite his better judgment, he always had thought less of the Ordaitian stock than he knew he should. For, while Galacia had the largest, most powerful, amazing navy in all the realms, Seamus knew that there was a reason that Tur'Mor of Ordiatea was the Heart of the Republic. Millions lived in those cities, their armies were innumerable, and their technologies were fast outpacing most of the known world. That being said, looking down on the lot of Ordiatian, Tuawtian, and Galacian ladies and lords, Seamus could clearly see where the power lay, and that was with the Captain of The Pearl of Red Duchess.

A tall, slender woman, whose skin was as dark as midnight and whose nose and mouth were concealed behind a veil of glossy red cloth spoke next. Seamus could barely make out her words due to the thickness of her accent. "High Captain Atura'poha'alana," she began, annunciating every syllable with a harsh click of her tongue. Though, to her credit, pronounced the foreign name of the captain with near-perfect precision. "What the pale man said is not wrong. We have given many funds to this ship for the going. We do expect to see our destination soon. We have not been told many words on our arrival time."

Seamus felt his heart leap in excitement. He had been hoping for this moment for weeks and weeks at sea. Carefully, he pressed his ear to the small hole, no longer able to see what was happening, but gaining a better quality of sound. He did not want to miss a word.

"You are well aware of what we seek," the Captain said firmly, her voice slightly hushed. "And you all know that we are not alone in our endeavors."

"Nonsense!" came a retort from an unseen male. "Who else even knows of the Goddess Heart?"

Goddess Heart? Seamus's brows furrowed. *What in Halfak's blazes were these people talking about?*

"Watch your over-grown tongue, sir!" The whip-like response came from a woman, Galacian by birth, obviously. "You have little right here to even speak. Men! O'ka-ufa!"

Seamus almost let out a laugh at the insult, of which he was sure the Ordiatian man missed. However, he was unwilling to remove his ear from the hole to look down and see the insulted man's visage.

"Lady Westport is right," the Captain spoke, referencing the title of the woman, denoting her Governess over the port city of Westport, as it was common in Galacian discourse. "We need not discuss such things out loud, even amongst ourselves in seclusion."

"Galacians and their secrecy. it is not well to hide truths from companions," came the voice of another, Tuawtian and male, his deep, throaty voice carrying much weight.

"We hold no truths, Vassal Und'Wak," Captain Atura said with surety. "We only seek to keep the nature of our journey concealed amongst ourselves. And I do believe we are all of one mind when it comes to the import of this thing, are we not?"

Seamus smirked. His lady, Captain Atura, was gifted with a tongue of silver. Even her normally heavy accent was mellowed out. And yet, she flowed from tone to tone as she spoke to each of the differing nations.

"The mighty Uuradan watch us well," replied the vassal. "That is true. But, we have not yet discussed *who* shall hold the Gift."

The room went silent. So silent that Seamus could not help but pull his ear from the hole due to discomfort. And despite the heat of his enclosure, he felt icy tendrils of worry crawl up his spine. Cautiously, he lowered his eye to the hole and searched the room once more.

A person, totally concealed in a purple robe was standing now, and all in the room were staring in its direction. A mask of solid gold concealed its face. A chain of gold, whose links were so fine Seamus was unsure if a needle could penetrate them, was laced about its neck several times, resting on the rich, purple cloth. A symbol, that of a circle inlaid with precious stones with rings winding about it time and time again hung from the center of the chain, a symbol Seamus did not recognize. The person, who was notably shorter than most in the room, though broad, square shoulders were apparent under the robes, had a sword at their side, whose hilt was bejeweled and the handle was of ivory. The scabbard of the sides-word was unadorned, save for a single rune, which looked to be a triangle with two blades crossing behind it.

"I do believe we are all acutely aware of *whom* shall hold the powers of the Goddess Heart." The masked person's voice was steel, unemotional, exact, and clearly discernible as female, though not feminine in the slightest.

Everyone in the room seemed to shrink before the masked speaker, unwilling to rebuttal the claim. And, with none to contend, the woman continued. "You were each selected for a specific reason, don't think to elevate yourselves above your station."

The fat Ordaitian man let out a *harumph!*

The side-sword flashed so quickly from its scabbard, entered the man's neck, and then slid across his vestments to be cleansed, that Seamus was not sure he had seen what he had witnessed. That was until the plump man rolled from his seat onto the floor, confirming the lethal strike.

"None are above my master." The sword hissed as it slid back into its scabbard. A note of finality rang out as the guard of the sword clicked against the golden locket.

"With all due respect, that was entirely unnecessary," Captain Atura snarled as she stared at the body, from whose neck a pool of blood was forming. "I am the captain of this ship and I will not have those under my stewardess treated in such a manner as this."

"I could cut the throat of your own daughter and have you proffered before me offering thanks," came the cold response of the figure in purple. "Each of you knows my master, and each of you knows of my loyalty to His Grace. His will shall not be impeded, not by the likes of any of you in the least."

There was another bone-chilling silence. Seamus felt the overwhelming desire to flee, a sensation that he was obliged to give into at the moment. Quickly, quietly, he shuffled back through the ventilation shaft, taking extra caution so as to not bump or scuff or otherwise draw attention to his concealment. His heart raced and sweat poured off his body as he slithered backward. He took short, fast breaths until his feet bumped against the wall at the entrance of the maintenance shaft. Seamus twisted about quickly and opened the hatch door that separated him from the Upper Deck.

Cool, salty air licked at his sweat-soaked skin, and rays of golden sun glistened off his body as he crawled onto the Upper Deck. He rolled over onto his back, slapping the hatch closed, and drew in several, long breaths. The sudden respite was cut short when Seamus spotted Master Charlie across the deck, shouting at a scullery-maid, waving his arms about in frustration.

Like an eel, Seamus darted away from the hatch, putting as much distance between himself and that ventilation shaft as possible. He had made it a good ten or twelve strides before Charlie had spotted him and shouted out, "Boy!"

Seamus went stiff as a mast, his arms flailing about as a wind-caught sail.

"Boy! Get over here!" Master Charlie was clearly not in a good mood.

"Aye, sir!" Seamus said, pulling up short from his run.

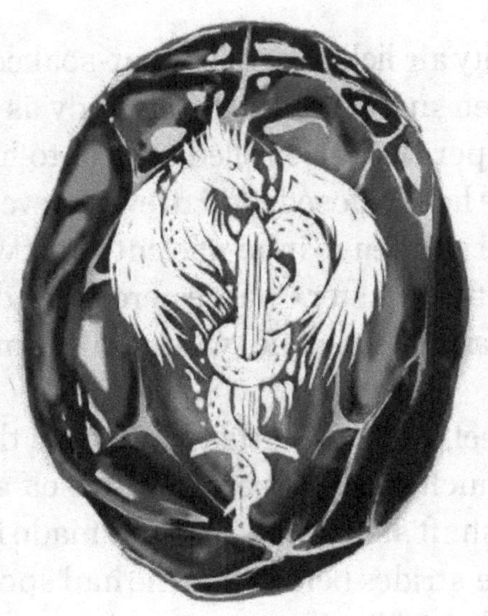

Chapter 3: The Mess

"Lightfoot!" Seamus hissed, leaning over the small bowl of piping hot stew, the steam mixing into the sweat of his lean, bare chest. "I'm telling the truth. Something strange is going on with this expedition."

"You worry far too much, Quickfingers," Henri said without looking up. He was studying a yellowed bit of parchment, holding a short, bronze magnifying glass up to his right eye and squinting something fierce.

"Did you not hear me, Lightfoot?" Seamus gawked. "There was some...*thing*, in a robe. It spitted one of the nobles, in front of the Captain." Seamus's voice was rising dangerously high, yet his fear of being overheard was being squandered by both his excitement due to the intrigue and his frustration with Henri's seemingly total lack of concern for the situation. "She didn't do a thing!"

"Really?" Henri said with a roll of his eyes, placing the bronze aperture he was staring through down on the table. "Seamus, you're my friend. So understand that, when I say this, I mean it in the nicest way possible. I simply do not believe you."

"What?" Seamus nearly threw his spoon in anger.

"Firstly, I think I would know if there were strange beings in purple robes lurking about the Pearl. Secondly, there are no weapons allowed within the vicinity of the Captain. And thirdly, my friend, and most assuredly, you are known quite well for spinning tall tales. And if you recall correctly, the last time I followed along I ended up scrubbing the decks alongside you. I do not wish to repeat that ever again."

Seamus threw his spoon.

The wooden utensil cracked Henri's forehead, splattering him and his paperwork with watery bits of meat and peas.

"What in Halfak's gates?" Henri swore, dabbing at the paperwork with a napkin.

"I'm not lying!" Seamus's voice was under less control than his actions. "And I'll be burned before I sit here and let you insult me! I'm telling you, something strange is happening on this bloody ship, and I mean to get to the bottom of it. I thought I could trust my friend to help me out."

The Mess went eerily quiet. Seamus felt his heart

sink. He would be striped for causing a scene. He would be forced to wear that infernal collar again - damned humiliating thing.

"I don't care what you think of scrubbing the deck," Henri yelled, rising quickly to his feet. "I'll not trade my place with you for three whole bars!"

Seamus blinked. Then the realization of what his friend was doing became crystal clear. He leaned into the argument, raising his hands and yelling, knowing that the punishment for arguing was mere separation, as long as it didn't come to blows. The punishment for being caught talking ill against the Captain could be as severe as being thrown overboard. "You don't do anything all day but sit and read! Maybe you should try an honest day's work!"

"Maybe you should learn to read!" Lightfoot shouted back, the corners of his lips pulling up into a tight, mocking smile.

Seamus let out a growl, "Low blow, but what else should I expect from someone who has to sit on a pile of books just to reach his plate?"

"Lads!" Master Charlie's voice cut through the commotion in the Mess like a hot knife through butter. Both Quickfingers and Lightfoot froze. They had been had, but hopefully, the crisis was averted. "If you two don't stop y'er bickering, I'm throw'n ya both into the drink, ya hear me?" the veins in Charlie's neck looked like snakes winding about a tree trunk and there was a fire in his eyes that could have scorched the sea dry.

It was not uncommon for the Master of Decks to have a temper, but Seamus noticed something else, something deeper, was behind his malice today. His mind immediately went to the secret council with the Captain. His stomach knotted when he pictured that sword skewering the rich nobleman.

"Out!" Master Charlie shouted. "Out or I'll find Fenron's Lost Blade and shove it up both y'er arses!"

"How would that work?" Seamus realized all too late he had spoken the question aloud.

The ear-ringing, open-handed crack to his face spun him around. Specks of white, green, and blue danced in his vision as a bout of nausea threatened his meal. Seamus clinched the table for support and caught the disapproving look on Henri's face. He seemed to be saying, *why? Why must you always do this? You do it to yourself, and you could avoid it every time.*

"Stuff it," Seamus mumbled, the hot taste of blood from a busted lip filling his mouth.

Lightfoot shrugged his thick shoulders, gathered his papers, and made as if to leave. Master Charlie apparently was not having it. He stretched out his hand and took hold of Henri's arm, thick fingers wrapping around with vice-like strength.

"We three are going to have a talk," Charlie said through measured breaths, attempting to compose himself. "Now."

The Master of Decks, while already gripping Henri's arm, took hold of Seamus by the back of the neck and led them from the Mess. Charlie swore wildly under his breath as he pushed them forward, knocking them haphazardly into the tables and chairs, sending their denizens sprawling, as he forced them out into the open air of the Upper Deck.

The sunlight assaulted Seamus's eyes, and while the Mess was by no means dark, being well lit by dozens of porthole-style windows, it was nothing compared to the open blaze of the sun at high noon. The deck shimmered with the haze of light, heat warping his vision. He went to rub at his eyes, but Master Charlie jerked him to the side, throwing both Henri and himself against the rails of the Pearl of the Red Duchess.

"I ought to have y'er tongues cut out!" He swore in a low voice. He thrust a meaty finger into Seamus's chest, leaned in close, and, through gritted teeth, breathed out, "Don't think I didn't hear you two arguing, or what y'er arguing about!"

"I-" Henri tried to speak, but was cut short with a stare so hot it could have melted all the Northern Ice Caps at once. He gulped in fear.

"Y'er gonna forget, boy." Master Charlie stated, fury seething from jaws that looked as if they could chew through iron. "Y'er gonna forget whatever it is ya thought you saw. Period!"

"Aye, sir," Seamus whimpered, not sure if he had pissed himself or if it was soup running down his britches.

"And you," Master Charlie turned his glare back onto Henri. "Y'er not gonna let this melon-brained halfwit try anything, or I'll skin y'er hide and fly it from the masts! Do you understand me, lad?"

Henri nodded so profusely that his spectacles fell from his head onto the deck.

Charlie stood up, eyeing both boys with a deadly expression, arms folded under his chest.

His bosom was rising and falling rapidly and his nostrils were flared like a beaten racehorse. Every hair on his leathery forearms stood erect and sweat poured from his brow, arms, and neck. He was not playing, he was not jesting, and he was not amused.

Something had deeply disturbed Master Charlie, and despite his own personal fear, this further intrigued Seamus. He could not help but feel validated in his curiosity. He felt the rush of adrenaline course through his body, and in absolute defiance of his better judgment, Seamus swore to himself he would figure out what was actually happening on this ship.

"I find out that one of y'er two-step one toe out of line, go poking around at rumors, or start snooping at all during the remainder of this voyage," Master Charlie stated as calmly as his shaking body would allow. "One single mistake, I'll have y'er both flogged, so help me Lady Gallae, I will have y'er both flogged until y'er meet the Goddess herself! Do. I. Make. Myself. CLEAR?"

And that settled it. There was no better way to get Seamus to do something than to expressly tell him not to do that self-same thing. And there was no better way to raise Henri's intrigue than to blatantly tell him to ignore some secret without any further explanation. That being said, both nodded in compliance, neither willing to risk another moment of physical abuse from the fuming Master of Decks.

"To your stations, lads. No more fooling about." Master Charlie's voice was clipped at the end of each word. He took a deep breath through the nose, and then let out a long sigh. "I don't want trouble, understand? Now, off with ya both!"

Chapter 4: Bow in the Wind

"It's odd, you know," Seamus said to Snapdragon, who was nestled in his arms, the sweet smell of perfume wafting from her thick hair, tingling at his nose.

"What?" she answered, not turning from her position, her hand resting on his thigh under the blankets.

"I mean," Seamus continued, unsure what he should reveal. "Do you notice anything strange going on with the captain?"

Snapdragon shifted, drawing her hands in front of

her, rolling her shoulder away from Seamus. "Quickie, you worry too much for your own good. A captain's business is her own."

Seamus, feeling the tension of her back and hearing the cool tones of Una'pahu's voice, decided it best to steer the conversation away from such murky waters. And what else should he have expected? She was in training to be a Ta'ala Gau, a Wave Guider. She was loyal to the Motherland and not any one man, especially not a deckhand of outlander blood.

"My Msa'oo," she whispered gently. "You worry about too many things. You cannot control the waves of the sea nor where they go."

"Strange sentiment coming from you," Seamus scoffed, running a finger through her thick hair.

"Ba!" Snapdragon laughed as she sat up quickly. The linen sheets fell off her body, revealing her tattooed, curvaceous back. Seamus gazed at the inky lines, following them from lean shoulders down to the small of her back. He reached out to caress her. She slapped his hand away and bent over to grab her huvu'huvu from the ground, the prayer beads clinking together as she wrapped about her bare waist.

"Going so soon?" Seamus said, lifting himself up onto one arm, still prone upon her soft bed. He didn't know which he would miss more, her warmth and touch or the soft, feather bed and smooth sheets.

"I am not a child, Msa'oo," Una'pahu said with

a false air of authority. “I have responsibilities to my title and house. Something you would not understand as a man-child.”

“Hey now! I am seventeen,” Seamus snapped, kicking his legs over the bed and reaching for his knee-length britches, all the while watching Una’pahu wrap her breasts in a long bit of cream-colored linen. “You don’t even turn seventeen for another six moon cycles!”

“Men are lesser, Msa’oo, even an outlander knows this to be true,” Snapdragon said as she patted him mockingly on the shoulder. She looked him up and down, a wildness in her deep, brown eyes. “You are lucky you are a fine-looking man, for being so pale. My mother would stripe me good for bedding an outlander as my first Msa’oo.”

In Galacian culture, it was not uncommon for polygamy. In all actuality, it was considered a sign of status and wealth. The more husbands a Wakatiti was betrothed to, the more responsible and powerful she was considered. That being said, the first Msa’oo was always a Galacian man, preferably a notable warrior or a head merchant. Seamus was neither of those things. Halfak, he wasn’t even a Galacian and he was as thin as a palm tree. Pale and lean, the ugliest form a man could be in the eyes of a Galacian woman. And yet, Snapdragon seemed to like him well enough, and that was fine by him.

“You know,” Seamus said as he threaded the rope through the belt loops of his brown britches. “I think my old man would’ve been proud had he met you.”

"Oh?"

"Yeah. I don't remember him much at all, but I remember he liked the sea and all that," Seamus's face reddened as he tried to articulate his feelings. He did not know how to compliment women. or talk to women if he was being honest with himself. He hadn't had a lot of practice before meeting Snapdragon.

Una'pahu turned and kissed him, a big, moist kiss, full on the mouth. She tasted of mango and coconut water. Seamus could have drunk her in for hours if she let him. But, this kiss had taken him by surprise. And when he gathered his wits about him he saw tears in Snapdragon's beautiful brown eyes.

"What's wrong?" Seamus asked, concern boiling up from deep within him.

"Quickie..." She began but then bit back a choking sob. "Seamus. The captain- Captain Atura has told me I am to focus wholly on my training as a Ta'ala Gau. She knows about us."

Seamus felt his world crashing in on him. This explained her distant behavior this morning. This also explained her eagerness last night. One of the two he was much less thrilled about than the other. A sickening bout of nausea churned within his gut. He licked his lips. They had gone cold.

"Seamus," Una'pahu's voice cracked. "I want you to know, you made me very happy."

"Don't say that," Seamus said as he reached out to touch her tear-streaked cheek.

She pulled back on instinct.

“We are done. You are an outlander and a deckhand. I am a Wakatiti and soon to be Ta’ala Gau. We are of two separate worlds. Two worlds which never should have come together.”

“Snap-”

“No, Seamus, don’t. I do not regret it. I loved you.”

“Loved?” Seamus felt weak. “I still love you.”

“No, you don’t,” Snapdragon choked out. “We loved an idea, a forbidden pleasure.”

“No!” Seamus found some measure of strength. “I loved you, Una! Damn it! I still love you! Why are you doing this? You can train and still, we can still-”

“No more, Msa’oo. You were my first love,” Snapdragon said, visibly steeling herself. “But no longer my Msa’oo. We are no more. Goodbye, Seamus Pearson. I trust you can find your way back to the Upper Deck where you belong?” And then she turned away from him, shutting the door in his face, leaving him utterly alone.

***

“I don’t understand,” Seamus whimpered. He was sitting across from Henri, his bowl of soup going cold in front of him, untouched.

“Quickfingers,” Lightfoot tread gently, peering over his spectacles at his friend. “I don’t know what else I can tell you. But, she had her reasons, didn’t she?”

“Reasons?” Seamus looked up, his eyes redden

with tears. “She gave me reasons. A bunch of garbage.”

“Listen, Quickie,” Henri tried to console his friend, but was cut off.

“Don’t call me that,” Seamus snapped. “I’m Quickfingers to you and Seamus to everyone else. It's just you and I now.”

“Alright,” Henri said, raising his hands in defense. “That being said. I do have some news to take your mind off it.”

Seamus looked up glumly, his eyes tempting Henri with an, *Oh really? Good news, ey? My love just left me and insulted my heritage, my birth, and my station in life. But please, do share some bit of useless information about numbers or maps or something*.

“I overheard that we’re pulling to port,” Henri said in a low voice, leaning over the table. “Turns out whoever that purple-robed person is, they want to pick up someone from Port Amandri. Supposedly it is a ways off from where the captain wanted to go. But, she apparently has no say so on this ship now.”

Seamus’s eyes glinted with something. A spark igniting behind their reddened sheen. And Henri knew he had him. True, heartache was probably a horrid thing, for those who were dumb enough to find someone to break their heart in the first place. But, Henri knew Seamus, he knew him well. And if there was one thing to take Seamus’s mind off of anything, it was secrets and mischief. Henri knew he might regret this later, but he needed to help his friend now.

"Go on," Seamus said, pushing his bowl of soup away and leaning over on his forearms.

"I overheard some of the crew saying that we were turning westward, away from where we were originally heading. Now, I have been looking at the maps, and the only island westward of where we are charted is Marblyn. And the only thing on Marblyn is Port Amandri, the last port of the Western Isles."

"Did you happen to hear who we are picking up?" Seamus's voice had a ring to it, the gloom melting away to intrigue. *Yes, this would work.*

"That purple-robed recluse doesn't let much slip," Henri answered. "Honestly, were it not for you telling me about them, I wouldn't have known that they were even on the ship. No, I haven't heard anything, but it's got to be someone, or something, important."

"Something?" Quickfingers asked, a quizzical look on his face.

"Now, before you go wild, well, just," Henri stumbled, trying not to overindulge his friend's imagination while still trying to get his thoughts out. "You yourself heard that we are looking for something, at least Captain Atura and this purple-robed individual are. Well, whatever it is, it's got to be something important if we are carrying such high-profile individuals onboard."

And that was the honest truth. Henri Sjo had been on many a voyage, and never once had he traveled with so many dignitaries of such varying origins all at the same time. He had seen together Zealots of Tuawtian, noble lords and ladies of Ordiatea, rulers of Calun, and even those from Eastern Zau'fi. They were clearly not comfortable around each other, but they seemed to have put their geographical distance, heritages, and religious belief systems aside for whatever they were searching for.

"They said something about a heart of some sort," Seamus whispered, unable to keep his voice measured.

Treasure hunting was not an uncommon pastime of the wealthy. As a matter of fact, many treasure hunters were funded by heads of households to bring back items of religious or historical note, only to have them displayed in the houses in glass cases or tacked to the walls of their manors. Henri did not understand the practice. He held the belief that these artifacts were not for others to take, and could not see how something so different made a house look any better. However, as his father had told him, *you can waste a lifetime trying to understand the motives of a rich man.*

"Seems like a lot of hassle for some heart," Henri scoffed. "They hunters?"

"Eh, what do you expect from rich people?"

"My thoughts exactly."

"That being said..." Seamus had a wry smile spreading across his lips.

Here it comes - the bad idea. The bad idea you

forced him to have, Henri, you bloody fool! What in the seven levels of Halfak were you thinking? It was only a little heartache. He would've been fine.

"What if we get it," Seamus whispered, leaning so close that Henri could smell his sour breath.

"Get whatever it is this robed person wants?"

"Yeah!"

"The same person who ran a noble through with a sword, in front of Captain Atura?" Henri's voice rose to a near bird-song pitch. He cleared his throat. "The same person who is now telling the captain where to sail her vessel, who is apparently over a dozen or so people from across the map?"

"Yeah," Seamus' eyes had widened with excitement as Herni had attempted to dissuade his friend.

He had only wanted to take his mind off of a girl. Oh, burn it all!

"You're going to get us both run through," moaned Henri. The tables had turned. Now it was Henri who was weary and Seamus who was consoling.

"Come now, we don't call you Lightfoot for nothing," Seamus said, slapping Henri on the shoulder. He rose, "How long till Port Amandri?"

"Three days," Henri groaned in reply.

"That gives me just enough time to make a plan!" Seamus beamed. "All I need from you is every bit of information you can glean!"

"Oh, is that it?" Henri said, standing next to his friend and looking out over the deck and on into the blue skies ahead.

"Come now, Lightfoot," Seamus said with vibrato,

placing an arm around his shoulder. "I think it is time for another ruse!"

***

A storm blew in on the second day from Lightfoot and Quickfinger's discussion. It was not a bad one, but the tempest was hard enough that Master Charlie did not force Seamus to scrub the decks, due to fear of a lightning strike.

Seamus was especially thankful for this, as it allowed him time to sneak about the ventilation shafts and snoop in on some very private conversations. He spied on two separate council sessions, both of which the purple-robed figure was absent. A disappointing fact, but it led to very promising information. It turned out that apparently nobody on the ship was happy about the presence of the masked person in purple.

Seamus had eavesdropped on a conversation between a Tuawtian Noblewoman, the same who had spoken during his first session, and a male from Calun, his coarse language easy for Seamus's native ears to understand. The muscular Calun man cursed the purple-clad specter, as he called them, openly. The Tuawtian woman was more reserved, though Seamus could tell she harbored ill will towards the shrouded being. They both spoke about the need for the being, but neither seemed thrilled where this 'Heart' was going, into the hands of the specter's master.

Another session placed Seamus above Captain Atura and Snapdragon. This conversation was far more painful for the other. He still loved her, and as he stared at her through a hole in the ceiling, he felt an uncomfortable sensation develop within. They were both very pretty, and he knew Una'pahu all too well. They were both dressed down into traditional Galacian wear, showing much skin in their huvu'huvu and wrapped chests. Captain Atura was leading Snapdragon through a series of motions. It was like a warrior's dance, each footfall firm and exact, while their hands moved in succinct motions.

Seamus was astonished by both the beauty and the fluidity of their motions. However, Snapdragon seemed to be frustrated. Maybe she was still thinking of him. Maybe she still loved him and it was all a lie. Upon further listening, he discovered that to not be the case.

"I cannot feel anything," Una'pahu panted, sweat rolling off her face as she strained in a crouching stance.

"Move with the waves," Captain Atura said firmly. She stepped solidly, yet gracefully, bringing both hands in a windmill fashion around her body. Seamus would have looked ridiculous doing the same motion, but somehow the captain looked mesmerizing with each motion she made.

"Yes, my Captain," Snapdragon answered. She regathered herself and then followed suit, moving her arms about and slamming her palms together before her.

A basin of water sat before them, rippling softly with the motions of the ship. Una'pahu focused on the liquid, eyes firm. Slowly, her body ebbed and flowed, bare feet sliding across the planks, lips moving silently. Seamus felt something a strange sensation, the hair-raising pulse of lightning before a strike. He leaned forward, gazing intently upon Una'pahu's dance. For the briefest moment, there was a subtle flash of green light and he could have sworn he saw the water in the basin lift, moving towards Una'pahu as if it had a will of its own.

The ship rocked with the waves, causing Seamus to knock his head against the wood beams of the ventilation shaft.

Captain Atura's head snapped upwards. She stared directly to where Seamus lay concealed. Seamus did not dare to move. He did not dare to breathe. He lay there, stiff as a board.

"Una'pahu," the captain snarled, eyes still fixed on the tiny, obscure hole in the ceiling. "Go to the Upper Deck. Get the deckhand with the red hair and bring him to me at once!"

"Ma'am?" Una'pahu sounded surprised.

"Girl!" Captain Atura snapped. "You are not Ta'ala Gua yet, and this is my ship! You will go now!"

"Aye, Captain! So sorry for the offense," Una'pahu said, bowing her head and backing away from the captain.

Seamus's head thudded in his ears so loud he

was certain that Captain Atura could hear it. A bout of thunder peeled outside, and another wave made the Pearl of Red Duchess creak. Timing the rise and fall of the waves, Seamus backed slowly, using the ship's own moaning to disguise his shuffling. He heard a door slam.

Seamus crawled backward as fast as his forearms and knees would take him. He felt splinters tug at his flesh, but he did not slow. He went back and back until his feet slammed against the end of the shaft. Whirling about, Seamus rushed up the ladder and threw open the hatch. Rain pounded against his sweat-soaked hair. The air, humid as it was, would have felt refreshing if his lungs were not burning with exhaustion. Across the deck, vision marred by pelting rain, Seamus heard the doors to the lower gully fling open. He slammed the hatch closed and dove across the ship's deck, crawling towards the rigging.

"Seamus!" Snapdragon's voice called out into the thunderstorm. There was an authority in her voice, but there was also fear. "Come here at once! Master Charlie said you were not below. Are you out here?"

Seamus, thankful for the cover of the storm, continued to crawl towards the rigging of the central mast. He laid low, hoping she wouldn't spot him. The rain soaked him to the core, and he left trails of blood from his forearms across the deck. Those did not concern him. The rain would wash them away.

He could see Snapdragon, hand held over her brow, blocking the downpour, peering over the ship. She walked forwards on unsure legs, the wind tearing at her huvu'huvu, prayer beads clacking together soundlessly under the tempest's fury. Long, arching, fingers of lightning reached across the sky. A boom of thunder shook the Pearl of Red Duchess, and a wave brought the bow of the ship upwards, pointing towards the sky.

Snapdragon tumbled overboard.

***

Icy water stole Una'pahu's breath away as she slapped onto the water's surface. A series of waves crashed over her, forcing her into the dark depths of the sea. Panic consumed her. Fear. Desperation. Fleeting thoughts of terror, echoed by flashes of ever dimming blue arcing above her in the sky. Una'pahu grabbed at her ancestral prayer beads, wooden circlets with green stones threaded throughout, and cried silently to the Lady Gallae for salvation.

A pillar of water rushed up from beneath her, slamming into her back and propelling her out from the darkening depths of the sea and onto the railing of the Pearl of Red Duchess. Dazed and not totally coherent, she felt herself slipping back over the edge of the ship. Not even the immense fear she felt could force her exhausted muscles into motion. Her head lulled as she began to slide back overboard, chancing a glimpse of a brilliant angel, wreathed in flames, soaring to her aid.

Pale, strong hands took her by her armpits. They glowed softly, veins bulging beneath the strain. She felt light-headed, as if in a dream. She looked up and saw eyes of burning green and she thought she almost recognized the face.

***

Seamus screamed. He drove his feet into the bulwark of the ship, his bloody hands gripping tightly at Snapdragon's limp body. She looked up at him, her brown eyes glazed over. A flash of lightning made it look like there was a hint of green deep within her irises, fading away.

Hadn't she gone overboard?

Seamus pulled with all his might, fighting against the rocking of the ship, the dead-weight of Snapdragon's soaked body, and the fatigue of his own body. One final yell, one final heave, and they both tumbled onto the deck.

He lay there for a moment, staring up into the sky. He had cracked his head good when they landed, and he knew there would be a knot. He couldn't tell if it was bleeding or not, his hands were already bloody and the rain made it impossible to feel any other sign. No, he did not even try to feel for injury, he laid there, heart pounding.

It's my fault. She wouldn't have come out here if I hadn't been snooping.

"Boy!" the familiar voice called out.

Master Charlie scooped up Una'pahu's body as swore under his breath. "Henri, get the boy out of the rain! Now!"

Seamus felt Henri take him under the arms and drag him below.

What have I done? Seamus shook his head slowly, *What did I see?*

Chapter 5: Gibbet

“What were you doing out in the storm?” Captain Atura thundered.

Seamus was sitting in a chair, in a room, with something wrong. His mind was fuzzy from cracking his head against the ship’s deck. He went to rub at the sore spot but found he could not move his arms. A surge of panic rushed over him. Was he paralyzed? He then felt the constraints tied about his wrists.

“I asked you a question, deckhand,” the captain snarled. “What were you doing?”

"I saw the, I um..." Seamus' tongue felt like lead in his mouth. "I mast the ringing."

"Master Charlie," Captain Atura, who had since put on her captain's uniform, turned on black, leather heels to face the broad man. "This deckhand is in your employee, is he not?"

"Yes, Ma'am," Master Charlie stammered.

"What were his orders, Deck Master?"

"Uh, ur, during a storm as this one, Ma'am, I don't have, er. What I mean to say is..."

"Well, spit it out! Or did you crack your skull as well, man?" Rage was apparent in the Captain's eyes, and Seamus felt somewhat glad that he couldn't muster a clear thought at the moment.

"He was on leave, Captain. The direction was to be below deck, Ma'am."

"Were you aware he was on the Upper Deck?" The captain asked through gritted teeth.

"No ma'am."

"And what were you doing instead of watching your deckhands?"

Master Charlie swallowed hard. His cheeks turned a ruddy color, and he spoke in sputters, "I, uh, was, well, indisposed at that time of the incident."

"Captain!" That was Snapdragon's voice. Seamus could tell she had been crying, though it sounded as if she was speaking into a conch shell. "Please, he saved my life!"

"Why were you out there, boy?" Captain Atura's voice was reaching a level of manic unrestraint, far from her normal controlled demeanor.

"I take full responsibility, Captain," Master Charlie said, standing between her and Seamus. "It falls on me."

Captain Atura's nostrils flared, and try as she might to see around the burly Master of Decks, he had positioned himself well between the two.

"Flogging," The captain stated coldly, placing her hands behind her back, the words barely escaping clenched teeth. "Ten lashings with the rod. Bareback in front of the crew. First thing in the morning. We make port by evening, and the boy will be left ashore. Dismissed."

Seamus, still tied to the chair, gazed dumbly at the door as it slammed behind Captain Atura. She had ushered Una'pahu out before her, who hadn't even looked over her shoulder at him before leaving. Several silent moments followed. Neither he nor Master Charlie spoke.

The Master of Decks, whose back had been to Seamus since he had stepped between his captain and his deckhand, turned slowly about. Seamus felt a lump form in his throat as he looked up into the weary face of a man who had just risked everything for him. He would be flogged for Seamus's stupidity. His mentor, his guide, and his leader, would be humiliated in front of the whole crew because he couldn't keep his own curiosity in check.

"Boy," Master Charlie's voice was low and raspy, and it seemed that he too had a lump in his throat. "You know what you did. I don't intend to ever cover for you again." And, without another word, Master Charlie reached behind Seamus and sliced through the ropes that held him bound. And then he left.

***

Sunrise brought the call of gulls in the air. Seamus rose from his hammock, sore and stiff. He rubbed his head. The sudden realization that what had transpired the night before, during the storm, was not a dream. A large lump had formed on the back of his head, and his fingers moved slowly over its bulbous surface.

"You up?" Lightfoot asked though he had clearly seen Seamus stirring.

"Aye," Quickfingers replied sullenly, though he didn't feel like 'Quickfingers' was a very appropriate code name anymore. Perhaps ass-mouth or dim-whit would work better.

"We best get up," Lightfoot continued. "The Captain made a call that all the crew should be called on the Upper Deck. Don't know what it's about. But, I reckon it's referring to going to Port Amandi."

"No," Seamus moaned, rolling out of his hammock.

Of course, Henri didn't know. He wasn't aware of this little escapade. No, this one was one-hundred percent Seamus's own genuine fault. No, Lightfoot was just studying maps and charts, reading potential clues. It was Seamus who had to go and actually do the bitter, hard work of spying. It was always him who was forced to do that kind of stuff.

That wasn't fair, and Seamus knew. But he hated that it was his fault that all this had gone south. They were supposed to go on a daring treasure hunt. Find some mystical Goddess Heart or something from right under the noses of those who were about to abandon him on Marblyn Island. To make it worse, Marblyn was a tiny spit of land used for cocoa production, housing only a single port. Who knew when the next ship would come through and offer him a chance to get away.

"You alright? I didn't hear you come in last night," Henri was studying Seamus now. "You don't look so good."

"Lightfoot," Seamus muttered. "I think I messed up, big."

"What did you do now?"

***

The crew was silent. The normal ruckus and obscenities that accompanied life about a ship was utterly absent. Only the crash of waves and the call of gulls were audible. It was a somber crew that Seamus and Henri walked out to see. A few hundred people stood, semicircle around a stockade. In that stockade knelt Master Charlie, back bared.

Captain Atura stood above the heads of the crew, atop a platform constructed of barrels and crates. She did not look happy about what was going to happen.

Seamus wasn't thrilled either. Master Charlie has sacrificed his own dignity for him, and what did Seamus have to show for it?

"There has been a spy amongst my crew!" Captain Atura shouted, looking over the crew in her dress blues, the feather of her tri-corner hat flapping in the breeze. "Due to negligence and lasciviousness, I charge the former Master of the Deck with neglect and debauchery while on duty. I sentence him to a flogging for his actions. Ten strikes across the back. Does the accused have anything to say for himself?"

"I willingly take my stripes," Master Charlie answered. "I take them for neglect, but not for debauchery. I also plead to maintain my title and seek the Captain's Penance for my actions, requesting twenty strikes and a week in the hold."

Captain Atura raised an eyebrow at the request and an audible gasp went up amongst the crew. Not since Seamus had first scored passage on the Pearl of Red Duchess had anyone pleaded for Captain's Penance. And to request additional stripes to boot. That being said, a noticeable softness crossed the captain's brow as she stared at one of her most loyal crew members.

"I accept your plea and grant you exemption from demotion depending upon terms of well-conducted behavior while in the hold," the captain said the words clearly. "I also will grant an increase in strikes, but not exceed fifteen. Marshal Weathers, be about your duty."

Marshal Weathers was perhaps the second most reclusive upon the Pearl of Red Duchess, next only to that masked specter in purple. Seamus shuddered as the broad, albeit short, Galacian man walked forwards from beside where the captain stood erect. His thick, curly hair was done up with wooden combs studded with veined-green stones. His broad chest and back were covered with black ink, as were his forearms, legs, and hands. His bare feet flopped on the deck and his tattooed fingers tightened around a rod wrapped in stingray skins.

The flogging was a horrid thing, and Seamus felt his guts in his throat. He watched the first six fall without flinching, trying his best to hold back. The next four were excruciating. And, despite an admirable show of strength initially, Master Charlie screamed out with each loud crack of the rod.

Seamus could bear it no longer. He surged forward, running faster than he had ever in his life. He leaped onto the stage next to the stockades and struck the Marshal across the face with a fist. An ear-splitting boom followed.

The world went black.

Seamus jolted awake in a panic. And when he looked out, all he could see was blue. When he looked down, all he could see were waves. And with a painful turn of his neck, when looked over, he saw the Pearl of Red Duchess, drifting alongside him, slightly blurred by the iron bars of a gibbet. Seamus was in every sailor's worst nightmare, hanging from a beam over an open ocean, confined in a steel cage, and left to die.

Chapter 6: Port Amandri

Pain, terrible and excruciating, racked Seamus's dangling body. Lines pressed into his flesh from where he leaned against the iron bars of the gibbet crisscrossed his body. The small cage looked like that of a wealthy noble's bird's cage, and felt to him not much larger. He could not stand within the confines of the cage, it was too short. Not only that, but the spaces between the bars were not wide enough for him to get a leg through. There was no reprieve from the constant ache of muscle and bone.

Dehydration had also set in, along with hunger pangs, sending him into a constant state of delirium. He saw visions of mermaids swimming beneath the deep. He saw gulls larger than houses fighting winged horses in the skies. Great sky eels wriggled about, snaring white whales in their tooth jaws. And a constant, dull thumping beat at the back of his mind, filling his brain with voices. There were Master Charlie's screams as the rod struck his flesh, time and time again. There was Snapdragon, telling him that she no longer wanted him. And then there was the disappointment in Henri's voice, telling him he was sorry that he couldn't save him.

"Land ho!" a voice called out from high in the crow's nest, atop the main mast of the Pearl of Red Duchess, amplified by a large conical device.

Seamus craned his neck about, the chain that held the gibbet had a way of constantly turning, so as to keep him from facing in one direction. What he saw brought tears to his eyes. Salvation was at hand.

A little more than two leagues ahead a mass loomed on the horizon. It was greenish grey and oddly shaped. Seamus, whose eyes he used to consider excellent but now were dampened due to staring at the burning rays for the sun, reflected off the glassy surface of the sea, knew that this strange lump was Marblyn. And Marblyn meant he would be sold off to work the cocoa fields, but it also meant freedom from this cursed cage.

"Seamus," a female's voice called out to him. "Seamus, can you hear me?"

Seamus rolled his head on an aching neck. To his surprise, he saw Snapdragon standing there. What was more surprising, was what she was wearing. What was she wearing? It looked to be an officer's cloak and trousers, and a tricorn hat.

"Seamus, can you hear me?" Snapdragon called out once more, and it sounded as if there was urgency in her voice. A look beyond her showed a deck full of sailors, moving about like bees at a hive.

"Aye," Seamus's voice cracked.

"Seamus, listen, I can't do much. But, I can do something," Snapdragon's eyes were darting about wearily. "Just, please don't say anything. Promise?"

Seamus stared dumbly back at her, his dull eyes drooping.

"Just, don't make a scene," Snapdragon's voice was near imploring. "I've, uh, learned something, recently, and I think it will help you."

She raised her hands before her, holding them so that the tips of her outstretched forefingers were touched, the back two twisting inwardly. She then touched her thumbs together and inhaled sharply. A soft tendril of green light swirled upwards, emanating from an emerald gemstone set within a strange, sinuous silver rod that hung from a set of prayer beads about her neck. As she inhaled the green mist, her eyes brightened as they had the night he had saved her from going overboard. She then blew out a breath and pointed her touching fingertips towards

Seamus.

A current of water wriggled from the beam that held the gibbet. It snaked its way towards Seamus, gradually picking up speed. Seamus panicked. He tried to push away, but his cage was far too small. A jet of cold water splashed into his face, drenching him, and bringing instant reprieve. Without thinking he lapped at the water, trying to catch it with blistered hands, still raw. Surprisingly, it wasn't salty nor was it brackish. It was cool, clear, freshwater.

"It's not much," Snapdragon said with a small smile, though she had turned her head away from him. "But you saved my life. The least I can do is give you a drink."

"I'm sorry," Seamus said, his voice pleading as he leaned against the cage. "I didn't mean to make any of this happen. I didn't mean to cause this."

"I know," Snapdragon sighed. "But you did it anyway. And that - that is why we cannot be. We are from two different worlds. I wish you well. I hope you will find peace."

Peace? Hope I will find peace? I'll be trapped, enslaved on an island. I'll be forced to labor every day until I die for another man's gain. I'll be alone. I'll be abused. Those were the thoughts that came to his mind, only after Una'pahu had walked away.

He threw his head back, cracking it against the gibbet, in the exact same place he had hit it on the deck. "Halfak burn it!" He cried aloud in agony.

"Burn it all," he sobbed, throwing his face into his hands.

***

The Port of Amandri was a small city set in a bay of breathtaking beauty. There were, however, no places for a ship the size of the Pearl of Red Duchess to land in its harbor, requiring anchors to be dropped and longboats let down so that a party could make its way to the city. Seamus, however, was not let down. The Marshal instructed him that they would be negotiating his worth, and a tradesman would be coming to claim him before they made to sail once more.

Hours passed, leaving Seamus dangling over the azure tides of Port Amandri. He stared at the white-sand beaches. The green foliage and the domed buildings that were carved into the cliffside crawled ever upward on the jagged rocks of Marblyn Isle. And of course, there were the gulls, squawking and shitting everywhere.

The twilight hours sent fuchsia rays of burning sunlight across the seas, which glistened gently, bearing no memories of the storms that had struck only days ago. The sky bled to purple, then black as stars rose and the moon crept ever higher. Despite all this, Seamus hung miserably in his cage, forced to observe one of the most spectacular sights that Ethrea had to offer in agony and despair.

Psst!

Seamus lulled his head towards the muffled noise. His eyes, bloodshot and dry, could barely make out the silhouette of a short, broad man, who had strange metal things on his face that reflected the moonlight.

"Oye! You still got quick fingers?" the voice strained, tempting the sound barriers of what one could call a whisper.

"Lightfoot?" Seamus responded lethargically. *What in the seven levels of Halfak was Henri doing here? He was supposed to be at Westerport?*

"Catch!"

As if snapping out of a dream, Seamus saw something whirling towards his face, end over end. His muscles spang to life and instinct overtook him. He threw his hand outwards, through the bars of the gibbet, and snatched the cold steel of a stiletto by its ivory and brass-pinned handle. The blade was about nine inches long, tapering gradually to a needle's point tip, and gleamed in the light like a silver flame.

Seamus eyed the stiletto with wonderment. However, when he looked up, Henri was gone. He looked across the deck, searching for any trace of his portly friend, but there was absolutely no sign of him. Turning his attention back to the blade, he noticed that the pommel of the stiletto was attached by threadings, allowing it to be screwed on and off. Daftly he worked his stiff fingers, turning the brass knob, revealing a small opening in the base of the hilt. Seamus tilted the knifepoint upwards and a pick-set fell out.

Seamus's mind raced over the series of outcomes his next actions could amount to. The main two that stuck both had to do with escaping now. Firstly, if he broke free of his cage, the swim to shore would be long and wearisome, forcing him to fight the moon's rising tide. And then where would he swim to? He couldn't swim into Port Amandri. No, he would have to swing left or right, swimming even further to find a safe place to beach. But what of rocks, jagged shards of death that line the looming cliffs of Marblyn Isle. But then what? If he did, the question was this, did he stay and try to make a life for himself, hiding in the forests of the upper plateau or did he hide in Port Amandri and seek to stowaway on the next merchant vessel or cargo haul?

These thoughts were dancing around his sun-baked mind as he squatted in his gibbet, gazing over the harbor of Port Amandri when he spotted lights reflecting from the water's surface. Far to the horizon, where the sun had set not long ago, faint, iridescent lights crept over the water's placid surface. They wove between a dark crimson into an even bleaker maroon, while rolling globs of black mists crawled slowly forwards.

Seamus gazed out upon the mirage, quite certain he had finally succumbed to dehydration and sun sickness. However, the loom lights and mists did not stall but moved ever closer to the Pearl of Red Duchess. And as Seamus stared, something horrific caught his eye. Rising like a shark's fin from the darkness, a mast with unfurled black sails seemed to form out of nothingness. And upon those sails were the markings every sailor, crewmate, and seafarer feared above all else, the crossed pistols and glaring eye of the Black Sister.

***

Una'pahu sat quietly beside her captain and mentor, her hands wrapped around her family heirloom, her birthright as the oldest daughter of her mother. There was a legend among her sisters, passed from mother to daughter for generations, that one day, one of her kinswomen would be called upon to awaken the power within this strange artifact. She, like her mother and her grandmother before her, and so on, had the ability to Touch the light within the stone, accessing the powers of the ancient Lifesource. Una gazed over the strange, muscle-like forms of the rod, running a finger over its unsettlingly smooth, yet veiny surface. The emerald in the head of the rod was a beautiful cut, and was probably worth more than three years of labor, though Una would never consider selling such an important bit of heritage. Family was everything to the true-blooded Galacian people, family, and tradition.

"But you do not hear me, Portmaster." Captain Atura'poha'alana barked. Apparently, her patience had run as thin as Una's attention. "You will provide as we agreed upon or Her Majesty, The

Goddess King Tunu'kuuna will set embargo upon you and your port. Port Amandri will shrivel and die!"

"You have no power to command here, woman!" The Portmaster spat back at her, as he folded long, dark fingers onto a rotund belly. His burly chest shone through an unlaced top of vibrant pink, crossed with sashes of gold and green. Matching sashes were wound about the top of his head, intertwined with wooden facsimiles of the Winged Ones, the ancient dragon goddesses of the Island Peoples. The shark-toothed-edged, wooden paddle, called a Buhna, that hung from his belt did not go unnoticed by Snapdragon. "You will meet my needs or we have no bargain."

"You are a dishonest, pig of a man! We agreed upon a price too high for your services anyways."

"Then leave without them," the Portmaster leered, showing crooked, yellowed teeth. He was a connoisseur of Cabyn leaf, which was obvious due to the rotting teeth and dilated eyes.

So, the fat Portmaster needed a high to confront the Captain? Weak little man. Una could not contain the chuckle. It simply burst out from her, richly ringing, howbeit shortly, in the small office.

"You need to keep a muzzle on your Artister dog, Captain," the Portmaster snarled as he turned beady, black eyes on Una. And then, to her great displeasure, he ran those eyes across her breasts and then down her body. He was nearly fifty, and the lust-filled glare made Una feel sick.

"You will not address a Wakatiti like that in my

presence," Captain Atura said, rising to her feet, hand going to her saber.

Four men in long robes of bright cloth quickly stepped forward from the back of the room, behind the captain. The Portmaster raised a hand nonchalantly, bidding them return to their posts, not a bit of fear or concern upon his face.

"It is my office," he said levelly. "I will speak as I wish. I have been granted the right to sit here, and you are a guest upon my shores. Remember that. Or do you not know culture?"

"Do not speak to me of culture, Kriv."

The Captain must be upset to use this man's name instead of title in a barter. Una watched with intensity. She knew that almost every deal would be met with a second barter, which was common amongst the Galacian peoples. But, apparently, there had been very strict negotiations done in place before this trip, and though Una didn't know all the details, it was painfully obvious that Captain Atura was not budging a fish's scale on them.

"So we dispense with pleasantries and go straight to the talk," Portmaster Kriv said, leaning back into his chair and pulling at the wispy thing that was attached to his lower lip that Una was sure he called a beard.

"The barter was set before the Pearl of Red Duchess set sail. We agreed upon payment for supplies and men for the work," Captain Atura said as she lowered herself back into her chair. She took a sharp breath and then sighed. "I cannot allow this not to happen. There are those on my ship who are heavily invested in this journey being a success."

"Ahhh, but you see," Kriv said with a dirty smile. "Where you seek to go, not a soul desires. It is cursed with a thousand curses, that island is. It is doomed with a thousand deaths. And the souls trapped there seek vengeance. My men, they are not eager to go. And our little island, there is so little for them to enjoy. The promise of," and he turned his eye back on Una. "Satisfactions will need to be made, for my men to take such a journey with you, of course."

"Kriv," Captain Atura snarled.

"You do not have to give up your Artister here, pretty thing as she is," Kriv said with a sigh. "But I am sure you have other girls that you could send to attend. Perhaps the little seabird wouldn't mind a night in comfort in my own bed?"

Ice ran through Una's veins, and the churn of her stomach nearly caused her to spill her guts onto the table. Even the thought of bedding this man made her nauseous, and the pain of her severing the relationship between her and Seamus made her want to strike the fat Portmaster. Her knuckles whitened around the silvery rod, and a cascade of emerald sparks crackled about the gemstone. When she turned her brown eyes on the man, she could feel the heat in her face- the anger, the embarrassment, the loathing.

"Ah, little seabird," the Portmaster chuckled. "You are cute. But there is not enough water here for your soft fingers to Touch. But, were you to spend the evening with me, you could touch many things."

A hand blurred through the air. It struck the jowls of the fat man, sending a ripple through his broad face. Una did not know what surprised her more, the fact that someone had struck the man or the fact that it hadn't been her. With wide eyes, Una turned and looked upon the tempestuous form of Captain Atura, leaning over the table and rearing his arm for a backhanded strike.

Before she could do so, thick, dark fingers wrapped around her wrists and shoulders, pulling her back. Three of the four men had grabbed her, and the fourth man placed meaty, calloused hands on Una'pahu's bare shoulders, sending a secondary chill down her spine.

"Now," Kriv said with wild eyes. "This one has fire, men! Perhaps she could fill the men's needs." He rubbed at his cheek, a purplish red welt was already forming. He then scrunched his lips into a pucker, drawing them up and to the left, as if it helped him concentrate. "On the second thoughts," his ascent bled through ever so slightly. "I do think we best listen to the lady, eh boys? Best not get under the wrong skirts, eh? These be stonefish in shallow waters. Best we tread carefully."

It took every ounce of constraint to hold her jaw closed. Una was shocked at the Portmaster's words. She was sure that both she and the captain were about to be forced. But why had he changed? She glared at him, jerking her shoulder free of the vice-grip of the man behind her.

"We will provide the men, these four, to take you to the farthest island of the sea, as agreed," the Portmaster said, the ascent melting away and a more business-like tone settling in. He then made a gesture for the guards to release Captain Atura, who in turn drew the chair out and sat rigidly, eyes fixed on the Portmaster with seething hatred. "Will you at least hold your end of the bargain?"

"You dare question my honor?" The captain scoffed, raising a thick eyebrow, sending the tattoos on her forehead into an arc. "After what you did?"

"I am confused. I merely sought to bargain, as acceptable. You struck me and I relinquished any further barter. What did I do wrong?"

Una could have sworn she heard her captain whisper, *Men!* Under her breath before continuing.

"As promised," Captain Atura said with a solemn voice. "Two of mine for four of yours. Pale skinned. It will be easy for you to keep an eye on them. They won't be able to sneak or blend in here."

The captain spoke in short, chopped-off sentences, doing her best to hide some emotion Una could not tell. But it hit her, the emotion, the description. *By the Goddess King's Throne! The captain was bartering Seamus and Henri for these brutes? Why?* Then, a thought even darker struck. *She had planned this before. Before the spying, the sneaking. Before the Pearl of Red Duchess had even set sail on this voyage.* Captain Atura had bartered away her lover's life for whatever it was that that purple-cloaked man was seeking, he had his gang of wealthy cohorts. Una felt a pit form in her stomach and the need to vomit almost overtook her.

"Is it settled then?" Captain Atura said coldly. "They will accompany you to your ship, and then you will send the pale boys back to shore with a few of my men. Have them in irons. I do not want disturbances. I run a clean operation. I would hate to... muddy the waters."

Captain Atura sniffed in mild displeasure and rolled her eyes.

How could she do this? She had known Seamus and Henri for years now? How could she sell them away? And for what? Some heart or something lost in a mystical cave? How could she even believe that?

Una'pahu poured her fears, her frustrations, and all her emotions into the rod. She tried everything she could to connect with that ancient spirit that was said to be kept within. She pushed. She drew upon the faint green light that pulsated with all her strength. But nothing happened. Her arm lost its strength and her hand, along with the rod, fell into her lap. She was going to lose Seamus for good.

Chapter 7: Darker Tides

Three lanterns rigged on tall poles on the bow of the longboats cast light over the dark waters of Port Amandri. Two dozen or so men were loading crates and barrels onto boats, filled with water, wine, and provisions for the rest of the journey. Una stood sulking, her slender frame leaning against an iron lamp pole when Captain Atura walked to her side.

"You handled that well," she said. "Better than me."

Una did not answer. She could not answer. How

could she? What would she even say?

"I am sorry about your friends, truly, I am. But, understand, I do not regret my decision. I have done what must be done. I need you to let go of your loyalties to them. Your place as a Wakatiti was always higher than to those foreign-born boys. You are a Ta'ala, daughter. Be proud in this thing. This is for the best."

"Yes, my captain." the words did not even seem to come from her own mouth, but Una had spoken them, respectfully- emotionlessly. She hadn't even teared up and choked on the submissive response. And she hated herself even more for it.

"You shall see," Captain Atura started, but her words faded as she gazed towards the lost horizon. Her brows furrowed. She pulled a looking glass from a leather holster on her belt, extended the brass aperture, and squinting one eye against the small end, turned it towards the horizon.

"By the Fenron's Blade!" She gasped.

Captain Atura whirled about. "Get the ship!" she bellowed to a group of stunned men, who each bore a mixture of uncertainty and fear. There was a breath's pause. Then, as if a whip had been cracked over their backs, they sprung into action.

Una looked to the men and then back to where Captain Atura had seen, well, whatever it was that she had seen. Nothing was there. There was only fog and night. Stars were still present in the sky.

Wait... fog doesn't move like that.

Una's heart flooded with fear.

***

"Black flags! Black flags!" screamed the watchman from the Crow's Nest. "Men to arms! Ready the cannons!"

What in the Forgotten Names of the Dragons? Pirates? This close to a port? That...that doesn't happen.

The gibbet suddenly felt very open. The bare exposure Seamus had felt, dangling over the open sea, up to this point seemed minuscule to the true dread that washed over him now.

"Help," the hoarse plea did not carry to the ship, Seamus knew this as soon as his parched and cracked lips had proffered up the cry. He was stranded. He was doomed.

Men and women alike rushed about like a school of silver fins before a barracuda. Deckhands were rolling barrels about and moving ropes and cords. Blue-coated soldiers with tricorn hats and long, smooth-bore muskets lined the railings of the Pearl of Red Duchess. They moved with a uniformity that was actually rather splendid. They pulled ramming rods from under their barrels and packed powder, patch, and ball down with affirmative action, eyes never wavering.

Pirates, upon the Western Seas, were not altogether uncommon, and these soldiers were no strangers to confrontation. These also knew that a typical bout with such a large ship was swiftly determined by the heavy guns aboard, not by the sharp-shooting musketeers. Seamus looked down and watched as several port hatches were lifted. Like an old badger sticking his head out to peer angrily at those who would trespass, black, iron barrels poked out along the ship's broadside.

The reports were deafening.

The gibbet swayed back and forth, and Seamus screamed as he clawed at his face, unable to silence the echoing booms of the guns. He cried as he stuffed grimy fingers into his ears, praying to all the gods he had ever heard of, both dragon and Ellitheor alike, that a shot wouldn't rip through his dangling prison.

Large splashes disturbed the bay, sending salty sprays high into the air where the cannonballs struck the water. Return fire soaked Seamus, washing the unpleasant scent of his fear from his body.

The brig that was approaching was doing so in an odd manner, slicing through the waves, bow pointed as if it were aiming to ram the Pearl of Red Duchess. At the bow, Seamus saw smoke rising from a tri-barreled long-gun. All three rounds that had hit the water had been fired from the said gun; despite his fear, he could not help but gawk at the strange apparatus on the front of the pirate's brig. It was not a normal thing, far too large, smaller than the nines on Pearl, perhaps sixes. But it moved on a swivel and crank, all copper, corroded and greened with brine. It was only after adjusting his eyes up from the tri-barreled gun that Seamus realized nothing about this ship was normal.

It had sails, furled and catching the wind, but cloth and nature were not its only propellant. Two large stacks, like the chimneys from a factory, puffed out smog, the self-same smog that had concealed the vessel. Something beneath the water churned, sending up wakes and pushing the brig faster than natural wind could take it. The brig looked to be totally formed of metal plates, riveted together in a tight form and painted black as night.

Panic, and the second report of guns, tore Seamus's attention from the pirate ship. He fumbled at the stiletto that Henri had thrown him- dear, blessed Henri. He would have to do something for that boy... if he made it out of this.

Quick as a yellow-tailed foxface, Seamus worked the fine tip of the knife into the lock of the gibbet until a subtle *click* sounded. The gibbet door swung open. Seamus looked up towards the Pearl of Red Duchess. No one was looking at him. He might have struck a named officer, but there were bigger worries than a deckhand at the moment. Every musketeer on deck was eyeing the oncoming vessel with hard eyes, muskets to shoulder and cheek, awaiting the command to fire.

Seamus tucked the stiletto into the back of his calf-length britches and crawled out onto the beam. Waves rocked the ship, the jolts of long-gun fire even more so. A shrill *whiz* was the only warning he received before a lead ball struck the side of the Pearl of Red Duchess, a mere arms span from where Seamus was crawling towards. Shrapnel sprayed outwards, accompanied by the screams of women and men who worked the guns. Seamus did not stop. He had to make it to the ship's deck if he meant to survive.

"Forward rank, kneel! Secondary, take aim!" Called out a broad-faced commander, her black hair braided and twisted into a tight bun on the nape of her neck. The entire front row of musketeers went down on one knee, resting the oiled wood of their muskets on the railing, and taking sight. The row behind them raised their long-barreled muskets to sigh, resting their left elbow into their hips for support. "Send'em to Halfak's hot gates!"

A wave of smoke bellowed out towards the oncoming pirate's ship, though it was the hundred or so lead balls that zipped through the air that would be their concern.

"One and Two, back!" Called out the commander, who stood proud as a statue. "Three and Four, forward."

And they moved.

Seamus, now back onto the Pearl of Red Duchess, searched about the deck for any signs of Henri or Master Charlie. He knew they wouldn't be atop, not during a fight. Neither were made for fighting. He needed to get below deck and find his friends. He needed to apologize to Master Charlie.

There were so many things he needed to do.

Boom! Boom! Boom!

Seamus was hurtled across the deck, dazed by a triple-blast of the brig's gun. It had been loaded so fast, impossibly fast. His ears rang, and Seamus thought that he could feel blood running from them. The upper deck was a shambles of blood and splintered wood, many of the Musketeers were torn to ribbons and strewn about in a horrific scene of gore and death. Seamus wanted to vomit, but he had no time.

The black sails of the brig were now clearly visible, a large crimson image of crossing sabers behind a weeping skull covered by a rent bridal veil. This was the terror of the Western Seas, the dreaded Black Sister. Seamus's heart dropped and his already parched mouth went dry. Everyone knew of the Black Sister, how only one survivor was ever allowed to escape the fate of their compatriots; and that said survivor would never live more than a few weeks at most after the attack, dying gruesome deaths from morbid wounds that festered and rotted away at them. But, it was those who had died at the hands of the Black Sister's crew that brought true fear. Bitten, torn, and gnawed upon, as if ravaged by wild beasts.

A bone-jarring crunch reverberated through the deck, toppling Seamus, and most of the musketeers, sending them sprawling on the sea-soaked Pearl of Red Duchess. The bow of the Black Sister had punctured the hull of the Duchess, a terrible brass skull with protruding fangs punching through the wood as easily as shot through glass.

Dozens of pirates swarmed over the ruined railing of the Pearl of Red Duchess, wielding sabers, daggers, small hatchets, tri-barreled pistols, single-shot dueling pistols, blunderbusses, and bidents and tridents. They were not in uniform nor were not orderly, like the musketeers who were scattered about upon the deck. They were fierce of face, heads of both men and women alike shorn and tattooed with red ink. Some were Tuawtian, that was certain, while others were of Galacian or Ordiatian heritage; however, there was something off about each of them, something that deeply unsettled Seamus as he stared up at them from his prone position. Their eyes were black, and not just their irises. Their skin was pale, despite some being nearly dark as coffee. It was a paleness of lifelessness, not of tone. It was a deadness of flesh, flesh that looks like marble or granite, not like soft skin. Some had bones that seemed to pierce the skin in strange places and others had long teeth and forked tongues. Others had lumps on their brows and skulls, like tiny horns pressing through cracked and black-veined flesh. They looked altogether horrific.

"Holy High Father above!" cried out Seamus as he stared on in horror and disbelief. He was not a particularly religious boy, to be honest, he had always felt the whole notion of religion was a bunch of contrived babble used to oppress. But, he had never seen demons before. And if there were demons from Halfak's own fiery gates, then it seemed reasonable, in the moment, to pray to a god above for some divine intervention.

A secondary volley of musket fire rattled Seamus's senses back, and subsequently dropped four or five of the rampaging demon pirates. Hot lead, smoke, and swearing filled the air as the pirates turned barrels and blades onto the secondaries.

Seamus, not willing to waste time by proffering up thanks to the god he had prayed to for salvation, scurried towards one of the many hatches that led to the Pearl's ventilation shafts. He crawled with weakened arms and legs, stiff with dehydration and fatigue, across splintered wood and jagged planks. He could feel the skin being torn and punctured, but he did not slow. He could see, just a few measures away, his escape.

"Boy!"

The voice was not human, it couldn't have been. It was far too perfect, too beautiful. Though it was pitched too high to be that of a woman's. However, when Seamus turned his head back to see where it had originated from, what he saw was every bit the body of a woman.

Atop the oxidized brass demon's head, stood a woman of breath-taking beauty. And the more Seamus stared at her, for he could not peel his eyes away from her ravishing form, the more he could feel himself become entangled in her seduction. She was not a tall woman, but she was very well endowed. Her face was smooth, and her eyes seemed almost too large for her head, offset by a tiny nose and thin red lips. Her hair, unlike her crew, was not shorn away but cascaded down to the small of her back in locks of blood-red hair. Not like Seamus's, not a natural red coloration for hair, but blood red. Her tongue pursed her lips, moistening them as it slid smoothly across in a hungry manner. Seamus did not like the way that made his insides turn, and yet, he had the strongest desire to go to her, as if all the will and fight within him had vanished at a glance into her maroon-haloed eyes.

Seamus felt as if he were a marionette, like the ones he had seen in Gal's markets, propped up by men in puffy-sleeved vests and colorful, tight britches. He stood without effort and began to walk dreamily towards the goddess. *What could be wrong? There is nothing to fear. She is kind. She is lovely. She will hold me, love me, touch me...*

"Come, boy, " she called out to him, so gentle, so caring. "Come to me now."

Seamus assumed the fight was still raging around him. People could have been shouting. There were definitely people dying, being blasted with lead-shot, ran through with cutlass and saber, hacked at with pike and ax. It was all so much, so vile, so devastating. And yet, Seamus simply could not be bothered by it. He felt detached from it all, as if it were a dream and he was merely lumbering through it.

"That's a good boy," the captain of the Black Sister cooed, as if she were speaking to a puppy.

A vibrant shimmer rippled through her maroon irises, drawing Seamus closer and closer to her. Her canines extended ever so slightly, forming into sharp points. They were lovely. Seamus felt a rush of heat burn up the side of his neck, causing his cheeks to flush.

"No!"

Something, or rather, someone, barreled into the captain, sending both tumbling down onto the deck. A bout of nausea struck Seamus the moment eye-contact was broken, followed by a flood of realization.

"What in the bloody-" Seamus started, bringing bloodied finger tips to his forehead.

"Ahk!" The cry of pain was sharp and short.

The captain of the Black Sister rose up from over a crumpled body, her perfect features drenched in blood. The blood of a large man with thick, hairy forearms.

"No!" The scream was Seamus's, though he did not realize it was his own. All he could do was stare in dumb horror at the lifeless body of Master Charlie, contorted in unnatural angles, blood running from his head, neck, and chest.

"Come here, boy!" called out the devil woman. She extended her hand, soaked in gore, beckoning Seamus forward. But whatever spell that had captivated him before was broken, and only hatred remained.

Seamus stepped towards her, acting as if he were under her spell. In truth, he could still feel the unnatural effects of her gaze, winding around his will as a constrictor slithers around its prey. But he was no longer the prey. He was the mongoose ready to kill the snake. He wobbled as he walked, and brushed into an overturned barrel, which knocked his right arm behind his back.

"Come, let me taste you," she mused, leaning forward and allowing her ample cleavage to show from beneath her low-necked blouse, bolstered up by a crimson corset with black embroidery.

Seamus drew near, trying his best to mute out the screams, blasts, and destruction that was taking place around him. He focused his mind. He steeled himself.

She reached out and brushed his cheek with a long, slender finger. It was not warm, nor was it icy cold. He felt a rush of something, like a shock of static, which flowed through his body, touching all the way down to his toes, forming a pleasant sensation. She stared down at him, her black eyes with maroon irises glistening in the moonlight.

Bells from Port Amandri sounded, chiming low and long in the distance. The pirates had been spotted.

The captain, if only for a second, turned her liquid-dead eyes towards the port, and Seamus seized the opportunity. He thrust the stiletto with all the strength he could muster. He drove the blade into her guts until he felt the hilt thud against her.

She gasped. Not out of pain, but out of

surprise.

"Oh, blackened fu-"

Seamus was cut mid swear off as she backhanded him across the face with such force as to lift him from the deck and send him flailing about wildly through the night air. He did not land softly. That being said, he had managed to cling to the stiletto. Or at least what was left of the knife. The entire length of the blade had been snapped off at the handle, and the only blood on it was his own, tricking slowly down numb fingertips. A throbbing ache began to pulsate in his wrist, and in his stupefied position, he wondered if he had broken it. As if that were his largest concern at the moment.

"You stupid little boy," came the alluring voice of the captain, though now it held a hard edge. "You could have gone peacefully into that eternal rest. But no, you had to go and ruin it. You looked so pretty. I do like pretty things."

She moved in a blur, so fast that Seamus did not have time to blink before she had a hand around his throat, lifting him up with ease. She held him in an impossible position, arm extended outwardly, leaving him dangling, though his feet flopped about the deck lamely.

"I could still turn you, make you mine," she mused, cocking her head ever so slightly and sticking out her rosy lower lip in a pout. A wicked smile curled the ends of her lips, not a pretty smile, but Seamus guessed it had the intended effect, for his body began to shake with terror as he dangled helplessly.

Seamus, realizing this might be his end, decided to make something of it, a final hurrah if you will. He swung wildly at the pirate captain, and his lack of any formal combat training showed with acute embarrassment. He missed her face twice, striking only open air. On his third mistimed flailing, the petite captain caught his wrist. Her fingers felt like a steel vice, digging into his flesh, bursting capillaries, and causing immediate bruising. The air was lurched from his lungs as a fist struck him in the guts.

She held Seamus there for a moment as if she were contemplating what to do with him while his body dangled. Then, with total nonchalance, she tossed him away from her. He struck the deck hard, tumbling over and over until he back slammed against one of the masts of the ship. A laugh escaped her terrifyingly beautiful lips. In the moonlight, she looked as if she were formed of glass, but Seamus knew all too well that there was nothing fragile about this demon captain. Her ink-black eyes, haloed with a maroon deep as sin, lit as The Pearl of Red Duchess burned around her.

Seamus could not stand. He tried, but his body was utterly spent. He laid there in agony as the captain of the Black Sister ambled towards another lifeless form, her bust in the open-paneled shirt swaying in perfect time with her curvaceous hips. Even in lieu of certain death, he was still captivated by her arcane beauty, every feature that of a predator, either meant to ensnare or kill.

However, it was the form that now worried Seamus, for that lump of flesh and cloth was none other than Henri. Anger boiled beneath Seamus' skin as she drew a short, single-edge blade from the scabbard at her waist. He needed to get up. He had to get up. He had to save his friend.

The report of a single shot rang out, accompanied by the sound of lead striking stone. The Captain of the Black Sister's head snapped back. And when it came back into focus, Seamus saw a slight trickle of blood emanating from a dark crack in her forehead, between the eyes. The flattened ball had not penetrated the bone, but it had ruptured her flesh. It fell with a clatter to the wooden deck between her leather boots. Seamus whirled his head about, searching for the source of the shot.

From an opened hatch the purple cloaked specter was stepping forwards with intense purpose. His left arm was extended with a tri-barreled pistol smoking in his gauntleted hand. In his right hand was a sword with a blade dripping blackened blood, and the golden mask over the specter's face was spattered with the same. A mechanical 'click' denoted the setting of the second barrel.

"Beatha'gha-"

The demon captain's unintelligible swear was cut off as a second lead ball struck her in the head, north of the first. This did not simply crack the bone but formed a crater in her flesh, shattered bits just managing to hang on to her bloody skull.

"Agh!" she screamed, dropping her saber and

grabbing at her fractured face.

"Back through the Dimdreal with you, Spawn of Sorrows!" cried out the masked figure in purple as it stepped purposefully forward, without any apparent fear. "I command thee to flee!"

A sound like shattering glass filled the air. The captain's body vanished in a puff of maroon smoke. Seamus's eyes widened with shock and horror. He craned his neck to look about the deck, propping his body up on his left arm. The purple cloaked specter was as still as a statue, though Seamus knew those coal eyes were darting about the ship with unnatural speed.

Across the deck, the hair-raising burst of glass shattering drew both Seamus and the specter's attention. Just above where two dead sailors lay, a swirl of maroon mist formed. The captain of the Black Sister struck with predatory speed. She latched onto the neck of one of the men with fangs of pure white. Blood splattered across the white shirt and blue coat of the dead man, and the demon devoured all she could. Seamus gawked, the wounds on her head stitching themselves together as she drank the poor sailor's blood, leaving not a trace of injury on her beautiful, horrifying, face.

A third shot rang out. This one, however, did not reach its mark. The demon captain moved in a whirl of black and maroon mist, vanishing and reappearing high in the air. She dropped from the sky in a streak, smashing into the planks, which cracked beneath her feet, splintering into thousands of pieces. Though, she did not fall through the upper deck, but floated mid-air, a spray of splinters twisting about her body.

"You dumb, foolish, little man!" She snarled, her voice was like velvet laced with poison.

A jet of water struck the captain of the Black Sister, blasting her from the sky, sending her crashing into the foremast of the Pearl of Red Duchess with a terrible thud.

Captain Atura and Snapdragon were both moving in absolute synchrony, each stepping with wide gates and solid footfalls. Their hips turned and their arms moved in wide, sweeping gestures. An emerald light glowed from about Snapdragon's eyes, twisting and winding like vines up into the air about her. She was chanting something, though Seamus could not tell what, and each time her mouth opened, tendrils of green light twisted into mist. At her waist, tucked beneath her huvu'huvu was a strange silver rod, in whose curling head was set a gemstone, whose gleam matched Snapdragon's eyes perfectly.

"Take them!" Screamed the captain of the Black Sister, who had swiftly regained her composure. "Take them and burn this useless vessel to its nails!"

Two dozen or so pirates rushed forward, some on all fours like animals, leaving behind the battered and bleeding musketeers. The feral pirates grabbed and snatched at Captain Atura and Snapdragon, whooping and hollering all the while. A jet of water blasted two of the pirates away, one of which was impaled upon a jutting sliver of wood. As the force of the blast, mixed with the pirate's own weight, forced his body to the end of the spike, the pirate screamed out in agony. He flailed and screamed, and then, in what could only be described as rapid decay, crumbled into ash.

For a long, silent moment, all was still. Everyone was motionless.

"I said take them!" Roared the red-haired woman, and even in her rage, stomping one of her thigh-high boots onto the deck, Seamus could not deny her luster.

Hands gripped Seamus, hauling him towards the Black Sister. He looked out over the wreckage, the carnage and death, and he felt a tear or two roll down his soddened cheeks. Atura and Snapdragon had tried to put up a fight, but they were eventually overpowered and shackled. Henri, whom Seamus had assumed dead, was being pulled towards the Black Sister by his ankles. He too was crying, just as weakly, just as hopelessly. Master Charlie was left, as were dozens of dead musketeers, whose bodies were strewn about in horrific angles. Seamus saw one of the pirates crouching over a musketeer, making a strange slurping noise. It made him sick. But what could he do about any of it now? He, just like the rest of them, were dead.

Chapter 8: Captive

The slow rocking of the waves woke Seamus, his head knocking against the iron bars of his cell. *Another cage.* Seamus was beginning to wonder what he had done in his life to have put himself in this position, yet again. That being said, being awake was not so bad. It was far better than the nightmares of that terrible night, watching his shipmates die and then, sailing away from the burning hull of the Pearl of Red Duchess, hearing those screams from those left aboard. Seamus held a half-hope that the Port

Amandri brigades had arrived in enough time to have saved some of them. But that hope was dim at best.

"How are you holding up?" Henri called out.

"How long have you been up?" Seamus replied, looking down at scarred fingers, wrapped expertly in clean, linen bandages. There was a sticky residue on them, some kind of strange concoction the pirates had used as an ointment. It had a strong, herbal smell to it that turned Seamus's stomach.

"I haven't slept. Can't." came the feeble reply.

Seamus had seen his friend sleep, never for long. Always in short bouts interrupted by screams and sobs. Each episode made Seamus's heart hurt for his friend. He had no desire to be in this situation, but he hated it even more, these pirates even more, for bringing Henri here as well. *It would have been better for him to die in peace with Master Charlie than to endure this.*

"Your head looks better," said Seamus as he stretched his aching muscles. "You can barely see the cut now."

It was true, the cut had been stitched deftly by one of the pirates, though Seamus could not have guessed why. That being said, the knot and corresponding bruise were not looking any better after three days of captivity.

"Still hurts royally."

"Guess it would, wouldn't it," muttered Seamus in a weary response.

"How are your hands?" Asked Henri

sheepishly, as if suddenly aware that he had been curt with his friend. "Are they healing?"

"Better than expected," the words came out in a halfhearted huff of a laugh. Seamus really had no clue as to why these pirates, who had killed without discretion mere days ago, were now bandaging and stitching together their captives.

"Odd, isn't it, Quickfingers?" mused Henri, running a finger over his seamed brow.

"Aye," Seamus replied. "Done been bandaged up for mealtime, I'd reckon." He said the words, and then immediately regretted it. Nauseating images from that fateful night wash over him, of demons kneeling over musketeers and sailors, slurping at their blood and feeding on their flesh. Cannibalism. A horrific thing- if these could be called cannibals. *Were they even people at all?*

"Will you two keep it down?" came the reproachful voice of Snapdragon.

Seamus turned his head over to look towards the Ta'ala Gau, towards Una'pahu Mue'Mora. She had once been the girl of his dreams. He had loved her, longed for her, day in and day out. But, she had changed. In truth, they had all changed, but she had really changed. Seamus could not unsee her moving the waves of the sea at her command. He could not unsee the green fire that had burned in her eyes. And he was terrified of her.

"We're simply talking," Henri spattered awkwardly. "Didn't mean to offend."

He had not seen what Snapdragon had done, but

Seamus had gone into explicit details of that night, how she and Captain Atura had commanded the waves. Una'pahu had corrected him there, stating that the captain had only been directing her and providing support, but that only she was a Ta'ala Gau, a Wave Guider. She went on some ramble afterward about how her great-grandmother had been the last True Ta'ala Gau in their bloodline and that some daughter of her mother's blood was destined to be a Ta'ala Gau, and that she had hoped it had been her before, but not now. She had always been a Wakatiti, and that had never bothered Seamus. But a Ta'ala Gau? Those were beings from legends, just like dragons and demons. It was all a little too much for Seamus, and when he looked at Henri, he felt as if his friend felt the same. Apparently, their indifference had offended her, and she had been short with them ever since.

"Don't go soft on her," Seamus chuckled darkly. "What, now she's got a fancy dress and corset on her, think you gotta listen to her?"

Snapdragon blushed.

She had been forced from her cage on their first night aboard the Black Sister, and when she returned, she was dressed in a scarlet skirt, a black corset, and a white blouse with little lacing to conceal herself. She had strange bruises on her arms and neck as well, though Seamus felt it best to not ask about them. Every night since then she had disappeared for a few hours and was returned again in a different dress. She would cradle herself, rocking back and forth in the back of her cage, and weep. It made Seamus sick. It filled him with rage and hatred. But there was simply nothing he could do.

"I didn't mean-" Seamus's voice broke, and he looked down at his bandaged hands. This was all so wrong, everything was all wrong.

"It's fine," sniffed Snapdragon. "Besides, it must be morning."

"How do you figure that? There ain't a single ray of light down here, save these weird glass lights," questioned Henri a little too eagerly, noticeably more relaxed with the shifting of the topic to somewhere other than Snapdragon's dresses and evenings.

"Well," Snapdragon said with derision in her voice thick as cold molasses. "These pirates never come out in the sunlight. They always make sure I'm locked away down here well before morning. I never hear any of them about during the daytime."

"Uh," relented Henri, a slight crinkle to his thick brows.

Seamus figured not realizing something as simple as waking patterns probably at Lightfoot like a mealworm. He couldn't help but let out a chuckle. Which, apparently, did not help decrease the furrow in Henri's brow, but rather deepened it and filled his face with frustration, pulling at the pink stitching.

"Ow!" cried Henri, raising a finger to the tender part of his forehead. "You'd think for a bunch of creeps who eat people, they wouldn't leave us down here."

"They're looking for something," Snapdragon stated bluntly, eyes fully focused upon the floor, boring holes between where her bare feet were planted.

"Wait," Seamus couldn't conceal the rising excitement. "You know something? Why are we down here? Where are we going?"

Snapdragon raised a cold, hard eye and turned it onto Seamus. "Quickie, this is not one of your childish games. We are in real trouble here. We are way over our heads, so I need you, and you, Lightfoot, to watch your tongues well with what I'm about to tell you."

Both boys nodded fervently.

"Okay," Snapdragon's eyes flashed between the two young men, and then she began with a whisper. "These things, whatever they are, they are searching for something in the farthest seas. They knew about us, about the Pearl, and why we were out - things I didn't even know."

"Like what?" Seamus was learning on his knees, face almost pressed through the cold bars of his cage.

"Can you not just listen, Quickie?"

"Sorry," he replied sheepishly, the forms of his very first smile in days creeping across his withered and soiled face.

"Apparently there is a hidden island, not charted or sojourned, far beyond the span of the Western Sea. And on this island, well, they said there was a relic of sorts. Something strange. They called it the Heart of Flame."

"By Fenron's holy blade!" swore Seamus, his eyes shooting over to Henri. "Lightfoot! It's what I told you! By the gods, these demons are after the same thing."

"Quiet!" hissed Una'pahu, glaring at her friends with fury.

Seamus noticed a halo of vibrant green surge around her irises, like waves crashing upon the black, jagged cliffsides of Westermost back home. He could not help but stare, mesmerized by their beauty, their light.

"What?" Snapdragon asked with hesitation.

"Your eyes," Seamus answered. "They are alive."

Snapdragon sighed. "Listen, Quickie. I know you and I, well, we had something. But I am Ta'ala Gau now, not just Wakatiti. I am different, changed. You must accept that."

"It's not that, I don't, I mean, I know," stammered Seamus, flushing a little at his own awkwardness. "What I mean to say is, your eyes, they are actually glowing, Una!"

"That means they're close! Hurry, pretend like you're asleep!"

"But you said they didn't come out in the day-" Seamus's retort was cut off by the squealing of iron hinges. The hatch opened slowly, letting in a beam of brilliant light, along with a breath of salty, but fresh, air. Something cloaked in shadows slithered down the ladder and vanished as the hatch shut with a dull *thud*.

Nobody moved. Nobody breathed. All were silent for several very tense moments.

But nothing happened. Noone assaulted the youths, nor did anything strike out at them. There was no maniacal laughter or taunting jibes. There was only silence, cold, unnerving silence.

"What do we do?" Henri asked, trying, and failing, to keep the tremor from his voice.

"Psst!" hissed Seamus. "We saw you come down the ladder. Might as well come out and show yourself."

"I am Wakatiti, Ta'ala Gau of the Goddess King's own service. I command you to show yourself at once!"

Despite the authoritative command, which Seamus was rather surprised that Snapdragon could muster in such terrifying circumstances, no one answered. No one alighted themselves from the shadows and spilled their secret plans. No one answered. Nothing happened.

"Well, what in Halfak's fiery gates do we do now?" whispered Seamus to Una'pahu, exasperation choking out his attempted curse.

"We hope it is not a Biter."

"A what?" Henri asked helplessly, all attempts at false vibrato gone from his voice.

"Well, I mean, they bit our sailors. Biters, Eaters, Feasters... I don't know. Biters just came out. We have to call them something." Snapdragon replied, her own confidence waning.

"Biters is fine by me," Henri replied quickly.

Then added, “Well, not fine by me, but the title is fine.” His eyes were darting about under his lenses wildly.

“Lightfoot, I am not sure what came down that ladder,” Seamus said slowly, quietly. “But I think that if it wanted to hurt us, it would have done so already. Maybe it’s trapped on this is damned ship as well, just trying to hide.”

“Maybe,” Una’pahu answered reassuringly. “But, I think we keep our conversations to ourselves and one of us keeps watch from now on.”

“I,” the voice was long and slow, like a distant echo in a vast canyon. “I am not your friend.”

The three friends all went stalk still.

“I am not of this ship, either,” the grave voice continued, somber and slow. “But I will not hurt you... if, *Cough! Cough!* ” The cough was wet and raspy, coming from deep within the thing’s chest. “If you do not mention me to the crew.” the finality in his voice spoke of the truthfulness of his statement, and Seamus did not doubt that this person was quite capable of hurting them.

“What do we do?” whispered Una’pahu with a trembling fear that was palpable.

“What do you mean, what do we do?” Henri scoffed. “We are behind bars. We can do nothing.”

“You can be silent,” the menacing voice in the shadows hissed. “You can be silent and you can avoid stupidity. The pirates of this ship are Biters, but that damned Captain Reylelan Trallae, she’s a bloody Turner.”

"A what," Lightfoot questioned.

"Hush!" shrilled Una'pahu, her green eyes burning wildly.

"Biters, they're no more than drones to their queen," the voice entailed, its slow hesitancy fading. "The people of Tuawtia, they call them a dark name, one which I shall not utter. But it is their queen that is the problem, and Captain Trallae, she is the worst of all Biters, for those whom her venomous fangs tear into are cursed to Turn."

"Turn?" Seamus questioned, being drawn into the conversation.

"Where do you think she got all of those Bitersfrom? They do not come so willingly before they're Turned," the voice echoed ruefully. "But once they Turn, they obey her every whim."

"That is ridiculous," snapped Henri. "I've never heard of such beasts."

"Did you not see? Were your eyes not open? Or else, how do you explain the loss of your whole ship?"

Henri did not reply.

"It is best we stop talking anyways," the gravelly voice cut through the silence with a bone-chilling harshness. "They'll be awaking soon, and you are not safe in the shadows."

"And are you?" Una'pahu asked in the false firmness Seamus knew she used when she was scared to prove she was not.

"No one is safe."

Chapter 9: The Captain of the Black Sister

Una'pahu, a daughter of Goddess Gallae, was led by those with fingers too long, skin too hard, and nails too black up the creaking steps of the Black Sister and out into the night air. The sky was dark, the crescent moon veiled by long wisps of opaque clouds. Biters loomed about the upper deck of the Black Sister, their too-large, black eyes dead, but ever-seeing, never blinking. They did not speak, each moving to some unheard beat to an unholy rhythm that chilled Una to the core.

It was a red velvet dress she wore this night, with a white bodice and ivory-boned riblets on her corset. It felt unnatural to her to wear such attire. Her whole life she had dressed according to the customs of the Wakatiti, never profaning her body with the clothes of the Easterners of Ordiatea and Calun. Her breasts, which were normally wrapped about tightly, felt as if they would pop out of the low-cut blouse if she took a wrong step or halted too quickly. Her hair too was done up in an Eastern manner, rolled and stacked high on her head. Face creams and paints had been amply applied to her, in a mostly vain attempt to cover her beautiful inkings, turning her rich skin to a near ghostly white. Despite all this, it was the shoes that bothered her most. She had worn shoes before many times, well, sandals really. But these things, these high-backed monstrosities were surely made as a device of torture, not allure. They made the simple act of walking nearly impossible, not to mention the sheer uncomfort that came from all the leather straps up her thighs and endless brass cogs and studs to boot.

"This way," wheezed a tall Biter, whose face looked to be slowly melting away from his bones. He wore tan knickers and a white blouse, whose laces were undone down the front, touting a particularly bone-protruding chest of ivory white.

"I know wh-"

Una'pahu was cut off by a sharp slap to the face which caused her vision to blur, filling her sight with white specks in the blackness that ensued.

"You do not speak unless told by Captain Trallae," droned a second Biter. This one was a thickly built female with sea-washed hair that was unkempt and knotted. Her eyes, like all others, were black, but it was the veins about them that were the most disturbing. Her's swelled and pulsated. It was a sickening sight to behold.

Una'pahu did not resist as they pushed her forwards, across the deck, and on towards the Captain's Quarters beneath the ghoulish helm of the Black Sister. Despite walking this same path each time she was summoned, the sheer eeriness took her breath away. The entirety of the Black Sister was horrific, from the gargoyles that perched to the demon faces carved into the beams, every bit of the ship was demonized and graphic in its design.

The Captain's Quarters was a large room, compared to the rest of the ship, adorned with red lamps and black candles. The mahogany table was stained with black lacquer and set with painted utensils. Two black marble statues of men, decapitated and hanging upside down on crosses, adorned the wall directly behind Captain Reylelan, who sat profoundly in a highbacked chair of red satin with black embroidery.

Captain Reylelan, as Una'pahu had come to expect, wore next to nothing. Her voluptuous figure was barely contained in a bodice that was laced up the back, and sheer across the bust. The trousers were nearly covered by a pair of boots that laced up her thighs in a way that made Una feel, despite her hatred, slightly jealous. The captain's figure was perfect, from the flowing locks of hair to her petite waist and curvaceous hips, and long legs. Her lips were stained with crimson, matching the shadow under her eyes and the blush on her ivory cheeks.

Two other men stood in the chamber, wearing nothing but leather straps about their groin, which wrapped around their rippling abdomens and bulging thighs. Their eyes, which were black and veined as the rest of the crew, were dead-locked on Una, staring hungrily at her. Una'pahu swallowed slowly as her eyes met theirs'. These two had not been present at any of the other meetings with the captain.

"Ah," Reylelan mused with a sickeningly sweet voice that reminded Una'pahu of those women who would call to young sailors at the dark alleys of port cities. "Welcome back."

Una'pahu did not respond, not vocally anyways. But she did feel that same strange alluring she felt each time the captain spoke to her. A chill crept down her spine as she felt her intuition haze. Her heartbeat quickened.

Captain Reylelan smiled.

A hand pressed firmly into Una'pahu's back, pushing her into the Captain's Quarters. Two more hands set her into a seat directly across from Captain Reylelan, who sat with her feet crossed atop the long table, reclining sensually in her own chair, not a concern at all on her porcelain face. A face Una'pahu had come to fear more than anything in the world. A face that haunted her dreams and filled her mind with dread during her moments of lucid captivity.

"Are you hungry?" mused Reylelan, cocking an eyebrow as she stared ravenously at Una'pahu.

"No," Una'pahu replied timidly. An intense pang of shame took Una by surprise. Why was she so mesmerized by this witch? How did she get in her head like this? Where was her spine?

"Darling, you need food. I would hate for you to lose your form," Captain Reylelan sighed. "You look absolutely delicious."

Una'pahu's stomach twisted and the sudden urge to vomit nearly overtook her. And yet, at the same time, a flutter of adornment blossomed in her breasts.

"You know what I like most about you, little one?" Reylelan questioned as she rose from her seat. "You have such strong will."

Una'pahu did not feel as if she had any will left at all. Part of her wanted to scream, to flee. And yet, like the effect of the Cabyn leaf on her mind, she wanted to melt into the witch, let her take her, let her-

"I can see it in your eyes," smirked Captain Reylelan as she leaned near Una'pahu's face, staring intensely into her eyes. The sweet aroma of apple blossoms and fresh rain filled the air. "You are breaking, my sweet. You are nearly mine. Ah... shall we begin?"

Dread filled Una'pahu's soul. *No,* she screamed inside her mind. *No! Not again. Please, gods no!*

"Boys," Captain Reylelan called over her shoulder. "Come here and hold our guest. I would hate for her to lash out again." she touched her cheek as she spoke, and a glint of amusement filled her eyes as she surely recalled Una's feeble attempt the night before. Useless.

Both men moved around either side of the table, the muscles on their bare torsos rippling with each step. Una had never seen men so built in her life, so strong, and- she shook her head, doing all she could to clear it. But it was too late. Their icy hands grabbed at her shoulders and arms, pinning her tightly to the chair.

"Now, where shall I begin?" Captain Reylelan's eyes burned with blackness so dark that all light was void within them.

***

Una'pahu ran as fast as she could, knocking over thatch chairs and baskets in her flight. She ran with a pounding heart, her vision blurred by hot tears that streamed from her reddened eyes. She ran and she ran, but the dread was ever-closing upon her. Through her mother's home she ran, past her two sisters' rooms and beyond the servants' quarters. She wept as she saw the blood-stains, the ruin of her childhood home. She screamed out in agony as she saw her sisters' lifeless bodies hacked to pieces. But she did not stop running, she could not.

Manic laughter filled Una'pahu's ears, reverberating off of the walls in sharp tones. Screams followed the laughter. Una'pahu burst around a corner, thrashing through the bead-doors that separated her mother's room from the rest of the house. She went stiff as stone.

Three beings, beastual things of black, inky-skin, stood around the bodies of her parents. Her father lay motionlessly, blood pooling from a gash upon his brow. Her mother, the High Lady of House Mue'Mora was stripped naked and bound with grimmy cords to her bedside chair. The mural behind her mother's bed depicting the Mother Isle, Gal, looked as if great claws had torn at it in a wild rage.

One of the three beasts, whose body looked more ox-like than the other two, who had appearances of avian origins, stepped forwards. Cloven hooves clacked harshly against the wooden floors as wisps of smoke rose into the air from where they burned. Its skin wriggled and writhed, as if something, or many things, were trying to escape from behind its unnatural flesh. A horn, long, spiraled, and silver jutted from his brow amid a series of red tattoos. The other two beasts also had horns in their foreheads, though not as pronounced as this one did.

The ox-like beast lunged forwards at Una'pahu

with lightning speed, swinging an unnaturally large hand with black talons for her face.

Una'pahu screamed out in horror.

"Ah," tittered Captain Reylelan as she stepped back.

Una'pahu's chest was heaving, and her body was drenched in sweat, but she was not in her mother's house. She was aboard the Black Sister. She was not facing massive, dark beasts, but a demon pirate witch. She had been taken back to the dream world. She had been taken back to Ymnathar, the Fractured Realm, where demons and monsters reside. Surely this was where Reylelan had slithered to Una'pahu's realm from.

"You guard your memories well, sweet one," Reylelan said as she lifted a painted fork from the table. "You are strong. I like that in my prey. It makes this all the more savory."

***

Una'pahu lurched upon the deck of the Pearl of Red Duchess. Heavy winds swept across the bow and tore at the tattered sails. Black waves rose high into the sky, maring the purple light with ominous ferocity. Icy rain bit into her skin, chilling her to the very bone.

"Snapdragon!" called a familiar voice.

Una'pahu whirled around the vacant deck, searching for the sound of the voice.

"Snapdragon, help me!" cried out Seamus.

Where was his voice coming from? Where was her

lover?

"It's filling up, please!" called out Seamus, though his voice was raspy now, as if he had been screaming for hours.

Something hard struck Una'pahu as she searched about the storm, the force of which drove her face-first into the deck. Una'pahu tried to get up, but whatever had hit her was now laying across her back, forcing her downwards into the wood planks. Warm, sticky blood seeped over her back, trickling down her arms and onto her hands.

A body!

Una'pahu forced her hands into the deck and heaved with all her might, rolling the corpse off of her. To her horror, Captain Atura's lifeless eyes stared upwards, her face twisted with pain as if all of this were all Una'pahu's fault.

Something on the deck flickered, something she had missed before. A smile, a sinuous bit of silver. It was something that Una'pahu knew, though she knew not how. It was long and straight, and at its tip, a bulbous green gemstone was wedged. From within that emerald, a pale light flickered. Una'pahu's eyes went wide with realization.

"Ah!" came the sultry voice of Captain Reylelan over the cast of the tumultuous storm. "You see it, don't you? Go, touch it."

Una'pahu, against her own free will, felt herself reach out towards the scepter. She knew it now. It was the totem her mother had entrusted her to guard. Something was very wrong. She should not be reaching for it. She should not touch it.

Why shouldn't I? Her fingers trembled as the cold metal reverberated at her touch. *It is mine. It was given to me to wield, to draw upon for strength. I can use it. It can grant me power to best this witch!*

Pulsating surges of energy washed through her soaked body. Warmth rushed through her veins, sending goose flesh across her arms, back, and neck. Una'pahu could feel the strength of her family's sacred totem invigorating her, she could feel-

No!

The voice seemed to scream out from within her very soul. It railed against her, fighting the urge to pull upon the power of the sacred totem. Una'pahu's muscles spasmed, causing her to drop the scepter on the deck of the ship.

No! Cried out a second voice, the voice of Captain Reylelan.

Why would she want me to touch this?

Una'pahu's vision blurred as a streak of pain rippled across her face. With marred vision, Una'pahu forced her eyes open once more. She was not upon the upper deck of the Pearl any longer. She was was in the Captain's Quarters of the Black Sister. Her hand was outstretched, her fingertips hovering a hair's breadth away from her mother's sacred totem, whose light was rapidly diminishing. Captain Reylelan was glaring at her, her own hand still in motion from the strike it had landed on Una'pahu's face.

"You stupid bitch! Why won't you touch it?"

Captain Reylelan screamed. All the sultry seduction had left her voice. Long fangs protruded from her mouth, drawing lines of blood from where they had punctured her lower lip, as if they had extended more rapidly than the witch captain had expected. The captain lowered her hand slowly, attempting to mask its manic shaking.

"You'll have to do better than that," Una'pahu slurred definitely. She lifted her head and stared the witch in the eyes. "You won't break me that easily, for I am a Ta'ala Gua of-"

A resounding crack rang out and all went black.

***

"I swear on the lost blade of Fenron, if they've hurt her," Seamus snarled, losing his words in a snarl of rage and a dream of violence. His knuckles had long since gone cold and white as he gripped the bars that held him.

"Quickfingers," Henri sighed hopelessly. "What would you do? Did you not see them? What they did?"

"I don't give a winged damn what these demons did or would do!" Seamus swore, wrenching his hands from the cage. "I'll gut them all, every last one of them!"

The hatch on the deck door shifted loudly, disrupting Seamus's tirade. Salty air washed down the opening and into the cramped chambers, followed by a series of footfalls. Two demons, strangely well built, and wearing next to nothing, hauled Snapdragon's lifeless body towards her cage. Seamus gawked in horror as he saw the trail of dried blood that stained her mouth, chin, neck and bosom.

"You bastards!" he screamed at them. "I'll kill you! I'll kill you all!"

They did not turn to face Seamus, they did not even acknowledge his threats. The two *men* threw Snapdragon's body into her cage with mechanized motions, unblinking, unfeeling. Then, beyond reason, they tore away the vibrant gown that covered his friend and once-lover, leaving her in not but her shift. One of the two then turned, cocking his head as he stared dead black eyes at Seamus, and then smiled a malice-filled smile. Seamus felt his heart go cold with ice and his flesh ripple with goosebumps.

"Our Captain would like you, little boy," mused the second, without even facing Seamus, as he folded the tattered dress. "She would enjoy your savor."

The two then left the hold, latching the upper hatch behind them.

"Well," Seamus heard Lightfoot say. "I'll help you, Quickfingers, if just to put a stake in either of their hearts... if they even have one."

Seamus stared at the hatch; hate and tears blurred his vision. A vice had set in his chest, he could barely breathe, but the rage he felt was a strong motivator. "We'll get our chance. And I have an idea that just might work."

Chapter 10: Blood for Blood

Two more weeks passed in much the same way as the prior days had. Seamus, Henri, and Una'pahu sat in their cages, rocked back and forth by the waves. Some nights the demons would come and take Una'pahu and others they would not. But when they did, Seamus would watch, he would count and he would plot. When food was delivered, Henri would seek out the bits necessary, he would hold them back and hide them. They didn't dare tell Una'pahu of what they were planning, it was too risky and she would surely try to stop them, stating it was suicide. But Seamus did not care if it was or was not, he wanted out of this hellhole and he wanted revenge on these pirate scum.

However, it was not just they two who were secretly working in the shadows of their confines. No, there was a third member of their little crew, one whom Seamus was not quite sure he could trust. But his options were limited at best. The Specter was there as well, aboard the Black Sister. It was he who had slunk below, and thanks to Hidden rations, had slowly begun to recover his health. Seamus had doubted it was the same at first, but stolen glimpses of purple cloth gave away the shrouded figure's identity or at least from where Seamus had seen them before.

"Boy," came the raspy voice from the shadows. "We are close now. I heard a bird's cry this morning. Are you ready?"

Seamus started at the sound of the Specter's proclamation, and a surge of anticipation invigorated his mind from his slumber. The weeks had passed slowly, but now that the moment was upon them, he could not help but feel the weight of the situation bearing down upon him. There were only two options, death or escape, and one of those seemed far more favorable to the other.

"How long?" whispered Seamus, trying his best not to awaken Snapdragon. Last night had been an especially hard night on her. She had wept for hours and her body was littered with bruises and knicks.

"Not sure," replied the harsh voice. "But not long.

Is your friend ready?"

Seamus looked over to Henri, who lay still in his cage, balled up around a white cloth and head leaned against the bars. Lightfoot had been with him for years. They were true friends. Seamus trusted him with his life, but did he trust himself with his friend's? A bit of dread found its way into his flow of excitement, bringing him down from the euphoric high of a well-laid-out plan.

"He'll do his part," Seamus stated, assuring himself as much as the Specter. "That I can promise."

"Good. We cannot afford gaps or missteps. Not today."

"Don't you think I know that?" leered Seamus. "It was my plan."

"Ha!" barked the Specter. "Your plan was gutter trash. Sure, I'll give you that it had good bones, but it was my suggestion that will get us out of this hellhole."

"You cocky prick!" gawked Seamus in utter surprise. "We'll see who ends up getting who out of where."

"Quite frankly, boy, I don't give a damn if you make it out of here or not," the Specter mused, and Seamus heard the being settle against a crate with a relaxing sigh as it spoke. "All I need is you to hold up your end of the bargain. And if you do, I will hold up mine."

Seamus scowled. He did not like this bargain, but he saw no other options. No other good ones anyways. "I'll do my part. But I swear on Fenron's lost blade if anything happens to-"

"Silence!" hiss the Specter. " They're coming."

"Wait," gasped Seamus. "We're not ready!"

"Hush!"

The rasping slide of metal against metal filled the darkened chamber, sending a child down Seamus's spine. They weren't ready. They hadn't time. Dread filled Seamus's heart as the sound of several demon pirates filtering down into the cell echoed about him.

Six of the Biters moved about stiffly, their dead eyes catching the moonlight from the open hatch. Two of them were lean and muscular, the rest seemed as if their flesh was about to rot off their bodies. Seamus wondered at this, despite his fear and frustration.

One of the two muscular Biters spoke up first, "Get the girl, leave the rest."

Seamus's gut clinched as it gave out orders; no harming or touching the prisoners. None of these things had ever spoken before when retrieving Snapdragon. They had always moved silently. Something was different. Something was wrong, and Seamus could feel it in the night's cold touch.

"Where are you taking her?" Seamus called out as the iron bars of Snapdragon's cage were opened and she was dragged out by her arms by two decomposing Biters.

"She has a purpose," sneered the second muscular biter, turning his angular face towards Seamus as he spoke. His black eyes seemed to sparkle, and Seamus felt as if he could stare into them forever.

He shook his head violently when he realized that Una'pahu was screaming as she was being dragged out of the cellar. "What are you doing with her?" He screamed again. But he was met not with another alluring stare, but a steely punch to the mouth, sending him crashing into the back of his cage.

"Our mother needs her strength," came the voice of the first to have spoken. "You will do nicely in due time."

"Or perhaps we shall have you," chuckled the second as he placed a hand on the bare chest of the other. Both laughed, a cold, wicked laugh and Seamus could see the hunger in their eyes.

"You two," the first commanded after he steadied himself. "Lock up and make sure nothing happens to them. Our mother wants them fresh for the journey ahead."

The scrape and turn of the latch atop the hatch of the cell reverberated through the darkness as the two Biters disappeared onto the upper deck of the Black Sister. The plan had shifted. This was not the way it was supposed to go. But Seamus felt his muscles tense in anticipation. At the end of the day, what needed to happen must go forward, and there was nothing he could do to save Snapdragon from here.

After several painstakingly long hours of silent waiting, Seamus noticed that the two Biters left on guard were utterly distracted. He took up a small bit of wood and flicked with speed and precision into Lightfoot's head, causing his stout friend to start awake. How he could sleep in a moment like this was beyond Seamus.

Henri looked up at his friend with a groggy expression as his left hand felt around for his spectacles. Then, with a jolt of awareness, Lightfoot sat upright and slid a bowl from under a loosened floorboard. Seamus sighed with guilt and remorse as he watched his friend quickly down the concoction. It was an act that nearly caused him to vomit, but he held back his desire to wretch.

"Uglk!" Henri gagged as he forced down the putrid sludge. He then slid the bowl under his buttocks and began to rock back and forth, his hands wrapped around his gut.

"Bless the gods!" cried out Seamus. "My friend, he's sick. Help him!"

The two Biters eyed Seamus with dead expressions, neither moving from where they now stood, not three feet away.

"Please, he is sick." Seamus pressed, a tinge of concern welling up.

Slowly, one of the Biters walked over to inspect Henri, squatting low and staring into his rapidly paling face. A face that turned from ashy white to putrid green in a horrific moment that seemed to slow in time. And then it happened. Like a volcano erupting into the ocean, Lightfoot spewed his guts into the face of the Biter, blinding his view and distracting him from what came next.

As a marlin screws its prey, the Specter darted

from the shadows, driving a fine-tipped rapier through the base of the second Biter's skull. The Biter did not have time to scream as its spine was severed, causing its body to disintegrate into ash. The first Biter, whose vision had been marred by Lightfoot's projection, whirled about, confusion and vomit plastered upon its face. Seamus, living up to his name of Quickfinger's, reached his hands through the bars that contained him and grabbed the demon, pinning it to the cage. With a swift flash of its steel, the Spector severed the head of the Biter, causing it to crumble like the other.

Surprisingly, the first part of the plan had succeeded, despite the extraction of Snapdragon. And what did they mean by *our mother needs her strength*? Seamus shook his head. He did not have time to think about that right now. No, now it was on to the dangerous part of the plan.

The Specter pulled the iron ring of keys from the pile of ash that was the first Biter. There were only three keys on the ring, so it took little time for him to release the boys. Henri, once freed, retched two more times, quietly as he could, expelling the distraction from his belly.

"You did good, boy," came the voice of the Specter as he wiped black blood from his blade. "And you didn't do half-bad yourself," he mused, turning his golden-masked face towards Seamus.

"What do you think they mean by our journey

ahead?" asked Henri, who had slowly been regaining the rudy coloration of his face.

"Something isn't right about all of this," Seamus added, helping his friend to his feet, but looking at the Specter. "Too many coincidences. From the moment they took us from Port Amandri, nothing has made any sense."

"Boy," the Specter rasped. "Focus on the task at hand. If I am not mistaken, we are near the farthest isle of the Western Sea, close to an island called in the ancient tongue, Duka'unka'falla."

"By the Winged Protectors!" Henri gasped. "Why would they bring us here?"

The purple cloaked being did not respond with words but reached its gauntleted hand under its robes and retrieved the lost stiletto. Seamus took it with a slow hand, sliding the slender blade into its sheath after examining it, then affixing it to his belt. The Specter reached a second time into his robes, this time revealing a flat blade that appeared to be a butcher's knife, but slightly longer and had an s-guard and joining nail upon it to protect the hand. He extended the weapon to Henri with a nod.

"We'll need all the help we can get now," it said with raspy tones.

"You didn't answer my friend's question," Seamus said stiffly. "You never said why you were here. You never even said why you were on the Pearl of Red Duchess. You are hiding something, and if we're in this together, we need to know."

The Specter stood silently for a long moment, his

shallow breaths the only noise coming from his masked face. Then, slowly, he let out a long sigh. "I cannot do this alone. My comrades died at the hands of these demons aboard the Pearl. Nor can I explain my purposes to you, not in full. You will just have to trust me. They will send more guards soon, and if we are near land, we must get off this ship or we will be nothing more than a trail snack for these cursed Biters."

"It's all connected, isn't it?" Seamus retaliated. "These things, where we're going, the secret meetings beneath the deck of the Pearl. It's all connected. By Gallea's Breath! It is, isn't it?"

The Specter, despite having its face covered, gave off an aurora of surprise. Then, a slight chuckle. "Boy, you have more wit between your ears than I gave you credit for. The Illuminated would be quite interested in you. But we haven't the time. All I can say is I was sent for a very specific purpose, and that purpose must be fulfilled. And despite our capture and misfortune at the hands of Captain Reylelan, I am still on course to succeed. Now, I need your help getting off this ship. If we can do that, and I complete my task, I promise, I will answer your questions. Do we have a deal?" Extending his left hand as a sign of trust as he finished speaking.

Seamus stared back at the Specter, a cold chill twisted about his spine but he saw no other way out of the current predicament. He had to save Una'pahu. Nothing else really mattered. Not secrets. Not legends or demons. Seamus would get Snapdragon back, even if it cost him his life to do so. He reached out and took the Specter's hand, shaking it in agreement.

***

Jacques moved quickly through the stacks of boxes and barrels, leading the two boys he had found through a maze he had come to know like the back of his hand, his left hand that is. His right, well, he had not seen that one in over a decade and a half. The golden mask he wore provided him with excellent vision, the tiny fragments of Lightstone within it amplified his sight and other senses to extra-human levels. So, it frustrated him that he had to move so slow, as to not level the boys behind him.

They were good boys, Seamus and Henri, a little presumptuous and somewhat pompous, but good boys nonetheless. They had handled their initial parts well, but it was still yet to be determined if they could follow through. Follow through; the hardest lesson any man must come to know. Jacques was a master swordsman, a title he did not come by easily. However, it was the title of The Hand of the Illuminated that had truly taught him the importance of following through, on not only sword-play, but in life, tasks, and duties. And he would see this mission through.

How had it all gone sideways? They had been so close. He had been so close. But more importantly, how did these Biters know of the girl? How did they find the Pearl? They had sailed directly to Port Amandri and struck with such an acute procession. They slaughtered an entire navy unit and dozens of trained musketeers. None of it was by chance. No, Jacques was sure of that. And this Captain Reylelan... Jacques had fought Biters before, but she was different. There was something more to that witch than he had realized. And she too was after the girl. Why? What could a Biter gain from her? More importantly, what could a Biter gain from the Heart? Dread filled Jacques's own mind as he poured over the plethora of circumstances that could befall them if a Biter were to get to the Heart of Duka'unka'falla. He could not – would not – let that happen. The implications were catastrophic.

Jacques opened the sword-shaped amulet about his neck that denoted his office of The Hand of the Illuminated. The sword was a facsimile of the Holy Blade of Fenron, the lost weapon that was said to be able to cleave darkness 136sunder. There were two, tiny gemstones within. One sapphire and one emerald, each set within the cross-guard of the blade. Both glowed, though the blue pulsated gently and the green arced like electricity. He closed the amulet, pressing it to his lips before affixing his golden mask over his face once more, and prayed that we would not have to use this tonight.

Captain Reylelan lounged upon silky sheets of rich blue. The bare flesh of her companions was hard and cold to the touch. She smiled as she ran a finger down the hard muscles of one of their stomachs, her eyes fixed on the Galacian girl tied to a chair at the foot of the bed. She was crying, a weak, muffled whimper that made Reylelan smile wider, tracing the pointed tips of her teeth with her tongue. The girl had a gag in her mouth, a cut piece of her own garments tied about her head. Reylelan loved to humiliate her victims, it was such a sensual pleasure, and she did love the pleasure of this realm.

"Girl," she mused. "Would you rather join us here? You look so uncomfortable."

One of the two male Biters, who was cuddled next to the other, rolled his black, veiny eyes. The other, traced his own finger down Reylelan's exposed thigh, as a ravenous hunger flashed in his eyes.

"Oh, stop it, pet," Reylelan said, swatting away his hand. She sat up, her long, blood-red hair flowing over her shoulders and barely concealed bosom. Her blouse was totally untied and the skirt she wore left little to the imagination, though she had kept on her knee-high boots.

"Mother," said the Biter with dismay as he rubbed at his hand. "We are hungry."

"Fine," replied Reylelan with exasperation. "Have the other one brought in."

Wicked smiles crept across the faces of the two Biters. The one closer to the side of the rolled over, exposing his nudity to the room without the slightest bit of shame.

These two are my best children yet. Reylelan contemplated as she stared at the near-perfect features of her slave. *So obedient. So pleasurable.*

The little, dark-hair Galacian girl turned her head away as the Biter rose. This caused Reylelan to laugh openly. "Dear, sweet, pet? Does the male form bother you so much? I will admit, it is not as smooth and supple as the female body. But, it does have its...benefits."

The girl muttered something, but it was utterly inaudible.

Inhaling deeply, Reylelan pulled from the oily darkness of Iodaba. The molten fumes of power streamed through her veins. It was an endless reservoir of power, infinite and eternal. A ringing sounded in her ears as she pulled the dark flows into her. A sound like shattering glass erupted as she directed a bolt, a maroonish black sliver of energy, into the gag that constrained the girl's tongue. The rag turned to ash, wisping away into the air. The girl let out a horrified scream.

"Come now, sweet," Reylelan cooed. The acidic taste of Iodaba tinged her tongue as she spoke, and the thrill of it caused her heart to race, though she kept a level head. Three hundred years of Touching the darkness had afforded her resilience to its luster. "Did you expect me to leave you gagged so that you could not speak? I just did not want you to interrupt me and my boys while we found pleasure."

"You're a sick freak!" screeched the little girl.

Tut tut! Reylelan clicked her tongue in feigned disappointment. "Such attitude is unbecoming of a member of the Wakatiti."

"Take my people's words from your filthy mouth, witch!" the girl railed as she struggled against her bonds.

"I believe you will not enjoy this as much as me and my children," Reylelan said as circled around the bed, walking directly behind the girl. She placed her hands on the girl's shoulders. They were soft and warm, so very different from those whom she had turned. But she could not turn her, not yet. She would, however, break her.

The side door to her chambers opened and her child came forward, dragging the body of a powerfully built Galacian woman, adorned with the ritual tattoos of a captain. The girl in the chair screamed out in horrified recognition as Reylelan's boys stretched the body over the bed.

"I believe this is your leader, is it not, my sweet?" Reylelan relished in these moments, and she could feel the hatred and fear boiling within the Galacian girl. She ran a hand across the girl's throat, dragging her long fingernails across the skin just hard enough to cause pain, but not draw blood.

"Captain Atura!" the girl screamed. Didn't she know where this would end? There was nothing she could do to save her, except...

The Captain was battered to near lifelessness. It was not how Reylelan would like to feed, but she was hungry, so very hungry. She could smell the salty, iron of the blood that pumped through the Captain's veins. She could see it pulsing, she could nearly taste it in the air. Her lip curled into a smile and she walked away from the bound girl.

"You have the option, child of the Islands," Reylelan said, forcing her attention away from the warm body of the captain and back to the girl. "You take this scepter and unlock its light or she dies. You have been stubborn for too long, and we have arrived at the Isle of Dragons' Fall. Touch the cursed light or she dies, and it is on your hands."

"Una," groaned the constrained captain from the bed. "Don't. I am dead already."

"By our Glorious Ones' power!" laughed Reylelan. "You can still speak? And you would give such poor advice as your final words?"

"Captain," the Galacian girl sobbed. "We'll get out of this. I'll-"

Reylalan slapped the girl before she could finish her useless mumblings.

"You don't get it, sweet," mocked Reylalan with a shake of her head. "You don't win this, you don't even know what this is. Now, I need you to touch the light from this scepter! I am losing my patience."

"The Ta'ala Gau are the protectors of the many waters," the captain shouted from the bed. "It was an honor to teach you, Una'pahu!"

Captain Atura thrust a leg upwards, wrapping it around one of Reylelan's concubines' necks, and twisted violently. A resounding crack resounded along with the motion, and then her boy fell to the ground, neck bone nearly jutting through his neck. Her other child thrust his hand through the captain's spine and out of her chest, sending a spray of blood across Reylelan's silk sheets.

Reylelan stared blankly at the scene, a bit of surprise, amusement, and frustration welling up inside her. On the one hand, she was impressed that the human woman could break the neck of one of her own children, especially in her current state. On the other, she had wanted to use the Captain as leverage to force the Wave Guider into submission.

"Well," she sighed. "No need to let our pet go to waste."

The Galacian girl screamed as her child feasted upon the flesh and blood. Reylelan walked over to the corpse, eyeing it with savage hunger. She reached out and grasped the scalding flow of Iodaba, forcing it into her body, and then channeling it towards the corpse.

To the naked eye, it would look just like black mist swirling about the corpse, but Reylelan could glimpse the power of Iodaba consuming the lifeforce of the fallen. She could feel it bring that same force into her own essence. It sustained her, strengthened her, and granted her powers beyond what this mortal realm could comprehend. She relished this feeling – craved it.

With trembling hands extended she drained the captain of her life, absorbing as much as she could into her own being. It was for this power that Reylelan had sworn her eternal soul, it was for this strength she had forsaken all else. A separate channel snaked its way towards the fallen body of her child. He was only a half-life being, but Iodaba must be fed, and so it latched onto it as well, draining any source of life it could from the once man.

"Ah,' sighed Reylelan wistfully, the black channels of Iodaba melting away. She smiled and felt that pulsing power of renewal coursing through her veins. And when she turned her eyes on the girl once more, she could finally see true horror.

Chapter 11: Sure as the Thunder

Seamus, Henri, and the Specter each darted their separate ways. They had their parts to play, and Seamus knew his well. As he slank alongside the underbelly of the Black Sister, he felt the cruel edges of a dark grin contorting his face. He would gut these demon pirates for what they had done to Una'puha. He would hear them scream and beg - he would snuff out their life - if these monstrosities even had life in them. Either way, he would end their miserable existence, of that he was sure.

The smooth handle of the stiletto felt cool in his hot palm, and the glisten of the steal seemed to croon for blood. *I'll carve the putrid flesh from their bones.*

To his disgust, the three were crouched over a dark form that could be nothing other than a body. They tore and ate at it, paying no heed to their surroundings, as dark blood stained the deck.

Seamus stopped short, concealing himself behind a rib of the boat, upon which a net and tackle hung. He studied the Biters, trying to piece out the best way to proceed. He needed to get to the guns, it was the Specter's job to free Una'puha, much to Seamus's complaints. The Specter had clearly shown, time and again, that he was the superior fighter. He was the only one who could contend with the Captain or her two lackeys. Henry was to have a longboat launched, making ready to row with all haste once Snapdragon was freed.

And I'm stuck disabling the guns, Seamus mused, contemplating the commands of the Specter. *So these bloody demons can't rain hell on us as we row away.*

A cold drizzle began to fall, mixing into the blood and grim of the deck. Seamus covered his nose with the back of his hand as the iron smell of gore sluiced toward him. The Biters did not seem to mind the rain, for low sounds of chewing and slurping emanating from their huddle forms did not slow in the slightest. Seamus's stomach lurched a second time as he watched from the net-strewn cove. The ship rolled over a wave - the sea becoming more tempestuous as the storm progressed - causing Seamus to lose his footing, knocking him to the deck with a thump.

The three Biters all lifted their heads in unison.

Shit!

Eerie clicking, sucking noises issued forth from their gaping jaws, which appeared to have been unhinged, slack and wobbling, dripping ichor and spittle. Dead, black eyes stared through the night, illuminated by a flash of lightning.

Shit!

One of the three, the tallest of the Biters, rose from its perched position. It had long, unnatural limbs, and where joints should have been, bones protrude from saggy flesh. The ghoul twisted its head, jaw still swinging slack as it walked, and glared at Seamus.

The stiletto felt minuscule in his hand as Seamus tried to rise to meet his foe. The blade's sharp tip punched through that warbling jaw, tearing easily through putrid skin, sinew, and puncturing bone. Black ichor and ghastly stench sprayed Seamus, whose mouth was open in a battle cry. Revulsion, followed by horror, rippled across his gore-soaked face. He vomited, and not a small amount.

The other two looked as stunned as Seamus felt, having not registered the fall of their comrade. This stupor, to Seamus's dismay, did not last long. As he was regaining his composure, using a frayed bit of his vest to wipe the gore from his face, the Biters began to stir. One of the two, an especially wicked-looking demon with crimson eyes and a jaw that split to reveal mandible-like protrusions lined with barbed teeth, opened its mouth and let out a chittering scream.

A surge of uncontrollable fear rippled through Seamus's body, rending his resolve to bits. Falling to his knees, Seamus clawed at his ears, doing all he could to stop the terrible noises that gnawed at him. Seamus was going to die - he knew it. There was no escaping this fiend.

A blast louder than cannon fire caused the whole deck to shutter, tossing Seamus into the wall yet again. He hit the wooden rib with a resounding thud, dropping the stiletto in the process. His ears rang something horrid, but to his near-immediate relief, the chittering scream had been utterly silenced.

"Gallae's tits," Seamus gasped as he pulled himself upright, his legs feeling little more than sacks of jelly that could barely support his weight.

The whole of the deck before him was a smoldering, ashen scar. Where there had been Biters, now there was charred bone. Specks of white danced in Seamus's vision and his ears rang wildly. A bolt of lightning had struck, drawn to the iron-barbed pole that other Biter had held.

"Shit!" Seamus yelled. And he laughed, patting at his unscathed body with frantic hands. "Holy Gallae, All-seeing Mother on High! Ha! I'm alive! How in the seven levels of Halfak?"

It did not matter. Seamus needed to move, and despite his current state, he had no time to wait and recompose. So, he hobbled away, stepping over the stinking, smoldering remains of those who he knew could have easily slain him had it not been for the most unusual bit of luck. And luck it was, for never in his life had anything so miraculous happened to him. Sure, he swore on the names of Gallae and Ordan, he cursed upon the Fallen Ones, and he even used Fenron's holy blade as a profane item to utter oaths upon, but in his heart of hearts, he had never actually believed in the Ellitheor.

Seamus ran down the deck of the Black Sister, slowly gathering speed as strength returned to his legs. He had to get to the guns and secure an escape.

Luck was too much. Seamus knew that. He had never been lucky. Not like this.

Damn... Don't go believing now. You'll have a slew of sins heaped upon you if you do.

The gods couldn't be real. They couldn't be. Right? But what of Snapdragon's gifts? Her unnatural ability to command the very waters. Men could not do that? That was all fables and children's stories, wasn't it? He had had time to process it all, to think it over. But he hadn't, not until now.

"Gods damn it all! I don't have time for this!" Seamus screamed into the rain and storms. His hands pulled at the rigging that held the guns in place.

Why now? Why this?

He had to get off this cursed ship. This whole thing was a nightmare. One long, horrid dream. He was asleep, swinging comfortably in his hammock, deep in the belly of the Pearl of Red Duchess. This rain, this fear, this blood, and these tears, this was all an allusion of his mind.

None of this is real. It can't be.

His hands fell from the ropes, the longboat still swinging over the storm-churning sea, black as midnight. Rain tormented the surface of the endless deep, pelting it ceaselessly, sending ripples over the foaming water. This was mirrored in Seamus's own subconscious. He felt ill. Tired eyes looked over bloody hands. If this was a dream, if this was all false reality, then he must wake himself.

But what if it wasn't? What if Una'pahu was trapped on this ghostship? What if Henri was fighting for his life? What if everyone was depending on him to provide an escape?

Don't be a gods damned fool, Seamus! No one has ever depended on you for anything. And if they did, you had let them down. Henri, you let him be beaten, just so you could have cheese and wine. Una'pahu, you let her take the fall for sneaking about, only because you knew that no one would strike a Wakatiti.

Two loud, resounding blasts tore through the storm's tempestuous fury, rattling the stupor that had fallen over Seamus's mind.

The signal!

Packing away the thoughts that assaulted his mind, Seamus worked at the rigging and knots, proving the title of Quickfingers to all those around him. Which was no one. But he did work fast, far faster than anyone could have expected in the wet and cold of the storm.

Within moments two of the long guns were pointed back into the Black Sister. Seamus worked as fast as he could, lining the inner wall with barrels of powder. There were sounds of screaming and gunfire now, all happening upon the deck above him. However, it was the next threat that reared its ugly head that caused Seamus's blood to run cold- though, it was not ugly at all. It was very, very beautiful- and utterly terrifying.

Captain Reylelan screamed.

Two blurs soared overboard, and Seamus thought he caught a glint of gold reflected in the night, sailing the opposite direction, just before they disappeared into the waves.

Frantic now, Seamus fumbled for dry fuses, sticking them into the back of the guns. But there was no match, no way for him to light them. Casting his eyes about, he saw a charred bit of hull that remained from the previous lightning strike that had so suddenly, and miraculously, saved his life.

Twice now? Seamus could not hold back a rye smile. *I might just become a believer*.

The hatch door that led down into the gunnery port was torn away. Not just opened, but ripped from its hinges, sending bits of wood and sparks flying. Rain and darkness were her backdrops. A terror of the night, Reylelan stood above Seamus with death in her eyes.

Seamus knew. He knew he could not get to that hanging bit of smoldering wood. He had seen Reylelan move. She was too fast, too powerful. He had failed, and he knew it. Seamus was going to die, and he was going to doom those he loved most in the process. The smile slid from his lips as the demon pirate began to step slowly downwards.

I guess not, eh?

A flash of brilliant emerald and sapphire light rippled over the upper deck, followed by a *whoosh* of wind. Reylelan's body was thrust against the opening, wood, and bone both cracking as she struck. Seamus, who beneath the deck was untouched by the blast, dove towards the chard bit of wood, red embers still alive, and ripped it from the hull.

Reylelan screamed again, more horrific than the first. Her mangled body was impaled by a bit of wood, pinning her to the narrow opening. Black blood dripped from her rent flesh as anguish marred her beautiful face.

Seamus, for a fleeting moment, felt an overwhelming need to go and free her. Concern, pity, and desire welled within his bosom. Holding the bit of smoking wood he walked towards the impaled captain. He looked up into her face, her perfect, wonderful face, and roared, "Shove it up your arse!" and touched the embers to the fuse. The double-shot thundered as Seamus flung himself through the charred hole and out into the abyss.

The water was ice cold, bitter with salt, and smelled of rot. The storm had churned up the depths of the sea, and the foam that crusted its surface, off white in coloring, washed over Seamus's face as he struggled to keep his head above the wake left by the Black Sister. The sea's rippling surface threatened to pull him downwards, but years at sea had given Seamus strong legs and a mind for treading water.

However, Seamus's prior dips into the sea had not been during a thunderstorm, nor had he been a starved prisoner in a gibbet only nights prior, or a captive of a demonic pirate queen... well, in truth, this was very different in every aspect.

"Ahoy!" cried out a voice in the darkness. "Is that you, Quickfingers?"

Seamus turned towards the call. He knew that voice. And though water battered at his ears, he could not mistake Lightfoot's nasally bellows. Looking back, he could see the Black Sister cutting its way forwards toward Duka'unka'falla and the Heart of which everyone was so desperate to find. Seamus could care less about a Heart or Duka'unka'falla. His lungs burned and his arms ached. It did not take long in clothes, even as scamp as his own, to get bogged down with fatigue.

"Pull him in!" the Specter barked.

Seamus felt hands grab at him, pulling him up out of the deep and over the edge of a small lifeboat. He flopped onto the dingy's wooden boards and puked frothy water and bile.

"You look like death incarnate," said the Specter through his golden mask, his voice raspy. His purple robes were sticking to his body, drenched with rain and seawater.

Seamus's eyes flitted about as he strained to gain his composure. Henri, shivering and soaked, was kneeling next to him. His glasses had a crack in the right lens, but somehow his friend had managed to not lose them in the waves. The Specter held at his side, doubled over in the front of the boat. He looked weak; he was clearly hurt. A flash of lightning illuminated the sky and Seamus could see blood streaming over the hand that clutched at his robes.

"Where is Una'puha?" Seamus asked, rising to his knees. "Henri, where is Snapdragon?"

Chapter 12: Gloves

"We have to get back to the Black Sister!" the boy shouted again, for who knew how many times over.

Jacques grimaced. He was losing too much blood to think clearly, to argue logic. He needed rest and to cauterize the wound. "Listen, boy, there is nothing else we can do for her right now."

"You! You said you'd save her!" Seamus screamed, tears running down his face. "I should've been the one to go, not you! Damn it! I trusted you!"

Jacques tried to breathe steadily, but every breath

burned, every gulp for life shallowed by the bullet wound in his side. He had had the girl, he had been so close.

"Listen to me," Jacques wheezed. This damned mask was making it too hard to breathe, but he needed it now more than ever, for, without the Everlight-powered stone set in the inner portion, he would have already died. He could feel the tendrils of Everlight seeping into his head, coursing through his veins, and attempting to heal the injury. But it was a dire wound, and the light was waning fast. "In my pouch, there's a Fragtorch. Crack the stone. You have to cauterize the wound."

"Why?" Seamus asked, his demeanor turning grim. "Why should we save you?"

"Quickfingers!" Henri protested, aghast.

Seamus shrugged his friend's hand from his shoulder, "Hold it, Lightfoot. Why should we save him? He didn't save Snapdragon. He is hiding something. Gods damn it, he is wearing a mask. What good has ever come from someone wearing a mask?"

"He saved me," Henri murmured. The lad was a kind heart one, Jacques could see that. It didn't matter. If they didn't stop arguing, he would bleed out. He hadn't the strength to draw the Fragtorch out now.

Seamus turned to his friend, "Did he? Or was it just another one of his illusions? We don't know anything about this guy! He could be leading us to our death!"

"You're being bullheaded, Quickie!"

"Don't call me that!" Seamus fired back, anger boiling in his words.

"I-"

"Una'pahu is on that ship and we're stuck out in the middle of the gods' damned sea in a thunderstorm. We're good as dead!"

"We aren't dead," Jacques growled. "But we will be if you don't save me."

Henri looked from his friend toward Jacques, his eye-pieces rainsoaked. His whole face looked sunken in, especially for one who had been so rotund when Jacques had met him. These two boys didn't deserve this.

What am I thinking? I have a mission. I must retrieve the Heart.

Henri turned back to Seamus and shook his head, spattering droplets of water falling from his soaked pate. He rose with an exasperating sigh and teetered toward where Jacques lay, bleeding out.

"In the pouch *cough cough!"* bloody spittle dripped down the inner parts of the golden mask, falling onto purple robes.

The boy - or young man, Jacques thought, no sense in treating them like children anymore - reached his hand unsteadily into the pouch and retrieved the silver rod with the gemstone set behind tinted glass.

"You have to crack it. It will burn hot and bright, but not long." Jacques groaned. "Everlight was never meant to be held so. Once you break it, stick it here." He lifted his hand, revealing an oozing hole in his flesh.

"Bite this." Henri's voice was flat and emotionless as he extended a chunk of wood.

"Can't. Don't worry about it."

"See, Henri," Seamus scoffed. "Damned specter won't even take its mask off. What is he hiding? Why are you trusting him?"

"He saved my life," Henri said, not looking back at his friend.

Henri took the Fragtorch and smashed the glass against the edge of the boat. A flash of vibrant blue light swelled outwardly, followed by twisting tendrils of misty sapphire, swirling about wildly. The stone, which had been set behind the glass, was burning hot, raindrops sizzling to steam as they fell upon its molten facets.

"This will probably hurt."

Henri thrust the Fragtorch into Jacques' wound. The boy was right. Damn, it hurt.

The sweet smell of cooking meat, mixed with singed hair and burnt cloth, filled the small boat with a horrifically-delicious scent. Screams and shouts followed. Jacques was pretty sure most of them were coming from him, but he couldn't be sure, not before the darkness took him.

***

"He is waking up," came Henri's voice over the crash

and fall of waves and the storm's fury.

"Good," Seamus groaned, pulling at the oars, though there was no happiness or relief in his voice, only misery and hatred.

"He saved my life," Henri grumbled.

"He left, her! He left Una'pahu," said Seamus, not looking towards his friend or the man in the mask he despised so deeply. How had Seamus trusted him so quickly? Why did he do what he had said? He should have gone after Una'pahu, he could have saved her.

"You didn't see them," Henri answered, his voice hollow and distant. "They had me, Seamus, they had me trapped and they were going to kill me. I saw him, he was about to go into the captain's quarters, but he saw me too. He saw them come after me, and he saved my life. They stabbed him and he still fought. They bit and tore and clawed and spat, and he fought. He fought to save me. And when I got the boat freed, he said he had a diversion, something that would distract them all. The next thing I know, he is running towards me like a wild boar, tackling me over the edge of the boat. And then there was only water and thunder. No more biting. No more terror. Only water. But, before we went over, I saw the captain's doors open. And I saw her, Snapdragon, alive. They need her for something, Seamus. They must. And we must not lose hope in that. We can still save her."

Henri's words were as the waves of the sea washing over the sands of the beach. They rose with a powerful swell, soaking the shore in its entirety. But as they subsided, only the coarse sand remained. Only

Seamus's coarse, hurting heart. He could not hear the words, not truly. He hated the masked man for not saving Una'pahu. But could he hate him for saving Henri? That was not right, that was not fair. Henri was his oldest friend, and to be honest, Seamus did not know what he would do without him. But Snapdragon, he loved her... didn't he?

Unable to find suitable words to deflect Lightfoot's words, Seamus grasped at the oars and pulled. He pulled and pulled, each motion burning the muscles in his back and arms. He pulled against the waves, against the storm, and the flood of emotions that raged within his heaving chest. Rain soaked his face, disguising the tears that flowed down his face. He did love Una'pahu, every stroke cementing that sensation deeper into his will. He loved her, and he would stop at nothing to get her back.

Dawn's rays brought the first signs of clear skies, low grey clouds torn by beams of golden light. Henri was leaned over the Specter, who was and had been asleep the whole of the night. Seamus did not look at his friend but through him. Something inside him had broken through the night. His deadlocked eyes stared sightlessly as he struggled against the sea.

"Seamus," Henri called out. "I- we're nearing the beach. We've made it."

Within moments the small boat slid into the white, sandy shores of Duka'unka'falla, the Island of the Damned. Tall palm trees swayed in the salt-tinged breeze, while colorful fauna and flora blossomed everywhere, a barrier of beauty just off the beach. A mountain rose out of the center of the island, whose peak emitted chains of twisting smoke.

"Its a volcanic island," Henri gasped, staring up at the towering, green mountain, whose lip was the only thing non-living. A halo of grey rock, like a crown, rested upon the top of the volcano, jagged and terrible.

"I don't see the Black Sister," Seamus grunted, attempting to hold back the awe he felt at the grandeur. He was furious, he was filled with malice and hate, but this was as nothing he had ever before seen in his life.

"Well," Henri scoffed, tilting his head towards the volcano. "If I was a cursed pirate demon queen, I would think of going there if I were searching for some heart."

"They won't be, not yet," groaned the Specter.

Both boys turned to look at the slumped man in the golden mask.

"They can't go out in the daylight," the man continued. "The sun burns their flesh."

"Then we find their ship," Seamus said, a spark of vengeance igniting within. "We sneak aboard and rescue Una'pahu."

"And then what?" the Specter scoffed. "What will you do then? Where will you go? Do you think to row this heap of boards across the Western Sea to Gal? I know you're young, but I didn't take you for a fool, Seamus. And what when night falls? What then will you do, when the demons prowl?"

"I'll cut their dead hearts from their rot core!" Seamus shouted in defiance, though he knew the Specter was right. What could he do? Was there no escape from this hell?

"Listen to me, and listen well," the Specter wheezed. "The Heart of Fire, it is here. The Illuminated One sent me here to retrieve it. All my original plans are dead in the sea, floating bodies no longer palpable. But, we are not dead yet, the three of us. If we can just get to the Heart, we can harness Its power. We could overtake the Black Sister and return to Gal. You do this thing for me, and I will grant you gold, I will free you both, give you land and names. You can marry Una'pahu, for I can make you both Par'par Mau."

"How do you know so much about our culture?" Seamus sneered at the weakened man.

"Your culture?" retorted the Specter, not even attempting to hide his rebuke.

"I have spent years under the banner of the Goddess and her King, High Lady Pylae Ono'fua Ma'mia Lo! I am as much a subject as any blood-born Galacian." Seamus answered definitely, though he knew he was not.

"But you are not touched by the Goddess, are you? You're pale skin and red hair will ever mark you an outsider. I cannot change that. But I can give you a name and house, something you could never achieve on your own."

"Even if I believed that you could do that, why

should I believe that you would?" asked Seamus harshly, though he felt a slight shift in his resolve, a crack in his proverbial wall of mistrust towards the Specter he had built. Never in his life had he ever seen a future for himself as more than a deckhand or second-rate citizen. The idea of having a name and a house was truly tantalizing.

"You don't have to believe me," coughed the Specter. Seamus could hear the blood gurgle in the man's words, the pain it caused him to speak. "But if you were to find the Heart, if you bring it to me, I swear to you on the Throne of Ordan and Gallae, upon my own life, that I will do these things for you. You do not know for whom I serve, but do this thing, and you will be rewarded."

The Specter reached into the pouch that had housed the now broken Fragtorch and retrieved a cylindrical tube of cast silver, whose surface was entirely covered with the forms of dragons writhing about. However, at the top, was the image of a man-no, a god. Fenron was depicted, standing high above the hoard of dragons, wielding his massive two-handed blade, flames dancing off its holy length.

"This is a map of the island. It will lead you to the Heart. I can't go with you, but I can give you this final aid and a final warning," the Specter said, slowly proffering the silver vessel. "Do not touch the Heart, for no man's flesh can stand the flame within. Take these," the Specter slid out a pair of odd-looking gloves. "Crafted from the flesh of the last known dragon to fly over Ethrea."

"You're joking, right?" Seamus scoffed, looking at the thick, scaly gloves, whose coloring was that of murky lake water.

"You swear by Gallae's holy name, you curse by the very blade of Fenron, and yet you do not believe in dragons?"

Seamus was silent. He obviously swore by Gallae, Halfak burn him, he swore by all the Ellitheor. Who else were you supposed to swear by? Was it even swearing if you didn't use their names? But believe in dragons, or actually believe in the Ellitheor? These were tales, stories, and myths. Seamus was no religious man, but then he had seen Una'pahu, hadn't he? Wielding the powers of her Goddess, Gallae, commanding the very waters of the sea.

Well, Snapdragon was a Wakatiti, she was above him, perhaps royalty could do such things. But dragons and gods? What was next, was this fool going to tell him that people could fly or cast flames from their very hands?

This was all becoming too much too fast. Seamus needed to rescue Una'pahu, not go on some damned wild goose chase through a gods' forsaken island in search of some burning secret heart. What was he even thinking?

"Listen, boy!" barked the Specter, a bit of steel coming through his pain. "You don't do this, we all die. You have seen what Raylelan can do, what she is capable of. If she obtains the Heart, it is my Order's belief that it would have compounding, catastrophic implications."

"So what, I just follow some treasure map to a mystical heart, waltz into the gods' know what kind of trap, and snatch up some kind of powerful relic that could, in the hands of a demon pirate, spell cataclysmic destruction?" Seamus scoffed, the words reverberating in his own ears with resounding ridiculousness.

"Yes," coughed the Specter, his voice having lost the hardness as he slumped back against the railing of the boat. "And before nightfall, if you could."

"Gallae's tits, what has this world come to?" Seamus said in utter astonishment.

"What other options do we have, Quickfingers?"

Seamus had totally forgotten about his contemplative friend, who had been sat upon his seat, thumbing at the beard under his chin. Seamus looked at him. *Had he gotten thinner?* Well, we have spent the last while in cages being fed next to nothing, so that makes sense. *Wait! What am I doing? Focus!*

Seamus let out a singular, hollow laugh. It died on his lips and he shook his head.

"Give me the gloves," said Seamus. "Henri, you've always been better with maps."

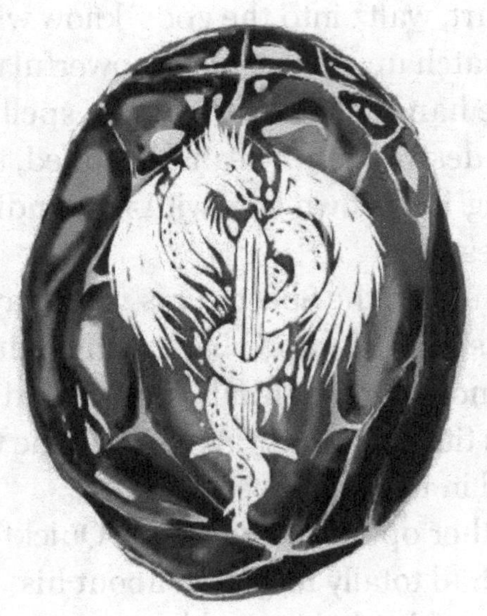

Chapter 13: To the Heart

Do you know what the absolute worst part of a jungle is? It's not the snakes, spiders, insects, or other living things that are trying to eat you, bite you, suck your blood, or otherwise annoy. No - although those things do make jungles miserable - it is the humidity. The relentless, hot, sticky, energy-draining humidity. And Seamus was absolutely furious with it.

"How much further, Lightfoot?"

"About ten minutes further along than the last time you asked, Quickie," Henri snapped back. He seemingly wasn't handling the humidity and constant buzzing of insects flitting around their eyes and ears and flying up their nostrils well either.

"I told you not to call me that," grumbled Seamus as he used the root of some foreign tree to help him climb the ever-steepening hill that was the base of the volcano. And of course, this Heart was going to be located in the volcano. Seamus hadn't even laughed about it when Henri pointed it out hours early when they had started their trek through the jungle.

"Then stop whining," said Henri. "I wish Snapdragon was here, just to shut you up. At least when she is around, your mouth is busy with things other than words!"

"Oye! Watch your tongue!" shot Seamus, though he could not help but feel the slight tug of a smile upon his lips. *When did Henri become the joking sort?*

"Then keep yours behind your lips. I have enough to worry about without you complaining all the damn time."

"Okay, okay," said Seamus.

"Besides, it's not like I a have pocket-clock or compass to measure time or distance off of," Henri continued, not even looking back at Seamus as he climbed. "Had it not been for the river's bend we crossed, I doubt we'd have any clue as to where we were. I can barely see the sun for all these trees."

Seamus shuddered at the thought of forging that river. They had to pick the leeches off each other, and Seamus hated leeches. Nasty, blood-sucking parasites.

"You're doing fine, Lightfoot," said Seamus consolingly. He knew how much Henri liked maps, charts, and compasses.

This whole thing must be doubly miserable for him. A stab of guilt pricked Seamus's conscience. He hadn't for one moment, up until then, even thought about how his friend was doing. Twice now, in one day, he was being mentally reprimanded for his treatment of Henri. They had been friends for so long, that Seamus had honestly begun taking him for granted. And this was more than the tricks that they had played upon each other when they were Deckhands upon the Pearl of Red Duchess. These were feelings of shame for not truly caring for the one who had been by his side, who had joked, consoled, and stowed away with him, even though he had had every chance to outgrow his bondage and become something more.

Seamus felt an urge, sudden and sharp, to say something, anything, to his friend. To thank him, to let him know how much he appreciated all that he had done for him. Halfak burn it, he was with him even now, climbing up a volcano to find the same Heart Seamus was seeking. Did he question or hesitate in the slightest to come along? No.

However, when Seamus opened his mouth, no words came out. His tongue caught and a lump formed in his throat. He wanted to say something to his friend, but he could not. He did not know if it was pride or embarrassment that halted his words, but they did not come.

On they climbed.

"Seamus, look at this!" exclaimed Henri.

The sudden outburst from their near-silent trudging sent Seamus whirling about, drawing his stiletto in a frenzy. But there was no foe, no assailant or malefactor. There was only Henri, who had stopped his marching and once again drawn the map from its silver canister, and was studying it with raised brows.

"Come here!" Henri called out. He then lifted his eyes, beholding Seamus's expression and drawn weapon. "And put that bloody thing away. It won't do you any good."

Seamus grumbled, begrudgingly tucking the stiletto away as he backtracked towards his friend, letting out a slew of inarticulate curses.

Henri, seemingly unperturbed by Seamus's lack of enthusiasm, unfurled the map and pointed excitedly. "Look! Here, no, not there, here, where I'm pointing! What do you see?"

"A line on a piece of paper," said Seamus with a heavy roll of his eyes.

"You- uh! Seamus, I am serious!" Henri said, crinkling the yellowed parchment as he pressed a thick finger into it. "Here. What do you see?"

"I, uh, well," Seamus mumbled, but then he actually looked at the map. The ink was strange. It glistened, unlike any ink he had ever seen before, tinges of emerald, sapphire, and some darker lines of onyx black seeming to emit a maroonish hue. However, this was not the oddest thing happening on the map. No, these lines were moving, forming into something more clear. "Is that a city?"

"Perhaps, maybe!" Henri affirmed, shaking his head in wonderment. "How...how do you suppose it is doing this? This could change the art of cartography, directly reflecting the interaction and relationship within the art and science of the process itself!"

"Wow, that is really something," Seamus answered with more than a hint of sarcasm.

"I am serious, Quickfingers! Think about all the practical applications! One could hide something in plain sight! Could disclose secrets that would-" Henri cut off.

Seamus, whose mind had already begun to wonder, snapped his full attention back onto his friend's rambling. No, not rambling.

"By Gallae's grace!" Henri gasped. "There's the path."

Both looked up in unison, scanning the terrain. The map's shifting face had depicted an outcropping of stone jutting out of the side of the volcano's slope. On the map, it almost looked like one of those mythological dragon's heads peeking out from its den where it hoarded treasures untold. Underneath that outcrop of rock, there was a pathway cut into the mountainside. When they looked out, trying their best to scan the ever-slopping mountain, they could not see more than a few feet due to the thick and leafy green about them.

"We have to get altitude. I can't see a damned thing," Henri sighed in aggravation, casting his eyes back down at the map and beginning to study it once more.

"I bet I could climb one of these trees here. Maybe breach the canopy and see something?" Seamus volunteered.

"Eh, what can it hurt," Henri said with a shrugging his thick shoulder, already disinterested in what his friend had to say, utterly drawn in by the markings on the paper he held.

Seamus shook his head and laughed to himself as he watched his friend find a spot to sit on an exposed bit of root. To the task at hand then. Methodically, Seamus searched about, seeking out the tallest, straightest tree he could find; a task far more challenging than expected. When they are upon the beach, tall, straight palms grew in abundance. Deep in the jungles of Duka'unka'falla, all of the trees were squat, thick things with twisting and splitting trucks and canopies.

At last, Seamus found a tree that he believed he could climb and gain somewhat of a vantage point. Years climbing masts and riggings had lent Seamus a knack for climbing, and in those self-same years, having earned the nickname Quickfingers well, he had gained an expertise in handholds and agility. It took no time at all to shimmy up the exotic tree, whose slimy bark smelt of citrus, and breach her massive green and red leafed canopy.

Seamus's breath caught.

Opening before him was a world unlike anything he had ever beheld. Endless, swaying green mirrored by vast blue skies filled his vision. Birds of various colors, shapes, and forms, many of which he had never before seen, fluttered at his presence, squawking and calling to one another. The desire to ride upon the winds as these birds did sang in his soul. The air, unstifled, smelled fresh. For the first time since trekking into the dense jungle, Seamus breathed in freely, the warm, sticky, salty air.

The scenery only engrossed his mind for a few moments before lucidity came crashing back upon him. He had not climbed this tree to sightsee - not for pleasure anyways. He had done this to seek out some strange landmark that had mysteriously painted itself upon a map. So Seamus shook free the thoughts of his mind and began scanning the volcano's sloping face.

It did not take long to spot the jutting outcropping of rock. as the map had depicted, the natural formation held an unnatural ambiance. It did look eerily like that of a dragon's head, or at least what dragon's had been depicted as in the books and fairytales Seamus had seen as a child. A massive snout with flared nostrils and spines forming a bristling mane about its curling horns. Veins and roots drooped off the beast's head and moss-covered its snout. The formation was not that far as the gull flies, but no less than an hour or so's march northwestward across the dense jungle floor.

Seamus looked to that azure sky and felt his heart sink. That blue would soon be tinged with the orange and pink of twilight's touch. There was less than an hour left before darkness would envelop the island and Reylelan and her hoard of Biters would be crawling over this volcano, like ants spilling out of a kicked hill. Gathering his facilities, and mentally marking a few trees, whose coloring stood out from the rest, Seamus scuttled down the tall tree and into the humid, thick jungle below.

"You see anything?" Henri asked, not looking up from his study of the strange map.

"You have no idea!" answered Seamus, voice uneven as he gasped for breath. It really was harder to breathe down here on the jungle's floor.

"What do you mean?" Henri stood, excitement painted across his face. "Did you find it?"

"Oh, I found it alright," Seamus answered, somehow already doubting himself and what he had seen with his own two eyes. "You wouldn't believe it, Lightfoot. By gods, what in Halfak's gates have we stepped into?"

"You're asking that now?" Henri asked with a raise of his eyebrow.

"Shit!" Seamus shout, reality coming back to him. "It's almost nightfall! We gotta go, now!"

"Oh?" Henri looked stupefied, but then understanding struck him as well. "Burn it!" He quickly he rolled the map and then stuffed it into the silver tube. "Where too?"

"This way," Seamus said. But he was already running towards the dragon's head.

"By Gallae's grace," gasped Henri. "I can't keep going. I can't breathe."

"We can't stop! The sun is setting," Seamus called out behind him, not slowing his pace in the slightest for his friend.

As if to affirm his words, a bellowing screech cut through the jungle's heavy undergrowth. It was long, horrific, and blood-curdling; unnatural loud and powerful. It was, if Seamus was not mistaken - and he did not think he was this time - the cry of Reylelan. But why? Why was she screaming?

Seamus, perhaps for the first time in his life, chose to do the smart thing and kept running. And to no surprise, so did Henri. Apparently fear of certain death was a great motivator to all mankind, regardless of build or athleticism.

They had to be getting close. He had passed the tree whose leaves looked like the massive fins of a sunfish, both in form and coloration. They had stumbled over the twisting roots of the crop of trees whose leaves were long and flat, hanging like a thousand swords, ready to slice and stab at them. And now, now they were nearing the thinning portion of the trail. The dragon's head would be - there!

Seamus knew that size was not everything, but this spectacle's size was unabashedly massive. From the tree tops, it had been hard to gauge size and distance perfectly. But he had not realized just how big the dragon's head would be. If he were a gnat, then this stony head would be the head of an ox.

"Gallae, Mother on High!" Henri gasped in awe, sucking breath in and out in great, labored heaving. "A dragon!"

Chapter 14: Shadow and Flame

Reylelan screamed. Fury boiled in her blood as she looked over the deck of the Black Sister, whose charred planks were as black as her name denoted. The sounds of creaking, straining, and moaning reverberated from beneath those planks. The sun was setting. It was time to release her children upon this accursed island and take what would surely place her at the right hand of her master.

A weak sob broke her glorious, indulgent fantizations of power and prestige.

Damn that stupid, sniveling bitch! Reylelan turned on her heels to see the dark-skinned whore slumped on the floor, crying weakly. Crying! Worthless, spineless waste of space. But she had needed her, she had needed her abilities to guide her here, to this cursed spit rock out in the middle of the gods-be-damned sea.

Torture is a beautiful thing. Brings out the very best. And despite her frustration at admitting it, this little girl had been far harder than she would have liked. Only in forcing her into the Dream Realm could Reylelan piece together how to get here. She had to peel away at her natural mind and see the Eye of the Sea. Of course, the girl had no idea what was happening to her, sniffling about, and crying for her friends. Bah! No, what Reylelan wanted was locked behind the mind of the living.

You see, only one of the Ta'ala Gau could truly commune with the sea. But each and every other Ta'ala Gau that Reylelan had captured had lacked the mental fortitude to withstand the torture long enough for her to see through the Eye of the Sea. But this girl, had something with her, that strange silver rod that gave her some kind of power Reylelan did not understand.

It was no matter, Reylelan smiled grimly. She looked down on the girl, chained to her bedpost, kneeling on the floor. Blood still coated the floor, both from one of her consorts and from that bloody annoying she-captain. Reylelan had a bitter hatred against the Galacians, a backward race of warp-minded ideologies. They were so concerned with their dead ancestors that they could not see the future unfolding before their very eyes.

The old ways were dead or dying. Too many people held on to petty ideas of family and culture. There was nothing to this life besides life itself, joy and pleasure. That was all, and then eternal nothingness. Only those who followed the great and terrible Khadais would never taste death, not in its fullness.

It had been over two hundred, maybe three - what did it really matter - years since a young, scared woman had forsaken her familial oaths, broken her marriage covenant, and followed after her new master. It did not even hurt anymore, to think about carving out her once-young love's heart and offering it to the Khadais as homage. No, nothing hurt anymore. She felt no hurt, nor pain, nor loneliness, nor sorrow. She had lovers, for none could withstand her gaze, she had loyal servants by the hundreds. And if she needed more, she could always turn them. This thought made were smirk, and the sudden urge to taste hot, thick blood sent a shudder down her spine.

"Wake up, child," Reylelan crooned, steeping over the Ta'ala Gau. "You have one last vision to show me."

The black-haired girl's eyes opened slowly, the lids sticking to one another, bonded by blood. Her pupils were dilated and unfocused, and bewilderment was the first expression that crossed her face.

"Ugh," moaned the girl as she rolled onto her back. The sound of dried blood pulling at flesh and wood crackled, a gruesome harmony in Reylelan's enhanced ears.

"I need you to focus, little Ta'ala Gau." the sweetness belied the malice.

"Burn in Halfak, witch," groaned the girl, the strain and pain in her voice arousing.

"Oh child," Reylenan said, brushing a strand of black hair from the girl's face with a gentle, cold finger. "I have burned. I always burn. But I live. I will live, I will live beyond the reckoning of time and eternity. And you will help me achieve this goal."

Reylelan inhaled deeply, sucking in the chaotic, bitter-sweet darkness that was Iodaba. The anti-light filled her veins, scorched her marbled flesh, and seared her eyes. She could feel the haloes of her eyes crackle with that beautiful, dreadful maroon. Blood boiled within and the air rippled around her, not as a stone thrown into the glassy surface of the water, but as a heat-haze on the endless desert sands. Stretching forth a finger, Reylelan touched the girl's forehead and opened her mind once more.

Reylelan did not know what torturous memories inflicted on the girl as she probed her mind, but she hoped that they were delightfully horrid. The worse the nightmare, the lower the mind's defenses. Reylelan peeled away layers of thought as the girl writhed and screamed, her voice cracking and breaking. The little bitch needed to stop that, she had not drank water in two days; she would have no voice left if she kept this up. Besides, the crying was distracting at the moment. Normally, Reylelan relished the screams of her prisoners, but this night was too important. She needed to get to the Heart.

A dragon swirled through the air, belching green flames.

A god soared, white-gold blade thrusting.

A mountain cried in agony, releasing molten tears over her tree.

A hollow formed, hidden by vine and root.

At its core, a Heart beat fire and life.

***

Una'pahu screamed as the icy, dead finger of the pirate captain scorched her brow. Waves of pain rippled through her mind, consuming her consciousness, and thrusting her into darkness.

Five women knelt beside her, forming a circle. They wore strange clothing, the likes of which Una'pahu had never seen. They each held in their hands a gemstone, pure and brilliant, which cast white light. Those that knelt, she knew them, somehow, though she could not discern from when nor whence.

But she did know them, didn't she?

In perfect accord, the five lifted their heads.

Una'pahu's breath caught.

Their eyes were not the eyes of mortal women.

They were vast and deep, endless pools of black, glistening with starlight. They had no irises nor pupils, just perfect blackness that glittered with an indescribable light. Under those strange, eternal orbs, beautiful tattoos were inked onto their crystalline flesh. And in their foreheads, a gemstone protruded.

Una'pahu had never seen such beings as these, but she knew in an instant that mortals they were not. In her youth, she had been told stories of beings from another world, another realm, who could, with their words, make mountains shake and oceans rise. That with their voices alone they could call forth fire and storms, shifting the very balance of nature. These were called the Heralds of the Ellitheor, second only to the High Mother Gallae and her family.

"Sisters," came the voice of one. "It is time."

"Sisters," echoed another. "Make ready."

"Sisters, join me now. For we must do what must not be undone."

"Join with me now."

"Together."

"Together," answered all. And to Una'pahu's surprise, so joined her voice in the proclamation. Though it was not her own voice, not truly, though it came from her own lips.

Vibrant, blinding light flashed.

The vision blinked away into darkness and Una'pahu faded into sleep.

***

Reylelan basked in the moon's pale light, high in the mast of the crow's nest, looking over her crew. Her children gazed at her with adoration. She loved it. Not them. But the adoration. She adored the love and devotion they proffered her.

"Tonight I attain exaltation! You will claim for me the Heart of this mountain," Reylelan pointed to the volcano behind her as she proclaimed her forthcoming victory. "We cut from this place her secret Heart, and I shall drink of its life."

The crew below her cheered with a veracity that rattled the beams beneath their feet. They stomped and shouted. They shook spears, hooks, and swords, raising them into the night sky in a chorus of praise and affirmation of her words. They would take the Heart for her, even if it killed them.

Reylelan flashed them all a smile, wide and wicked. "Tonight, we turn the course of history! Tonight, I seize the power of the ancient ones and gain the favor of the great Khadais!"

Like ants streaming from a kicked hill, her children spilled over the deck of the Black Sister, rushing the white, sandy shores of Duka'unka'falla, the Island of the Damned. The island that would gain her eternal life and name her the Right Hand of Khadais. Reylelan leapt from the crow's nest and soared out into the night, tendrils of Iodaba leaking from her flesh, trailing behind her like a cloak of ever-dark mist.

Chapter 15: The Dragon's Maw

Seamus Pearson's eyes watered as the acrid scent of sulfur burned his nostrils. The smell was near-unbearable, and he, not for the first time since leaving Port Amandri, thought that he would die from inhalation of noxious fumes. Lightfoot did not seem to be faring much better. The once rotund, spectacled lad, had tears welling in his eyes and leaking into his now rather impressively grown beard.

Despite the smell, the two pressed further into the winding, cavernous maze, formed by what looked to be ancient rivers of molten rock. Henri held the Fragtorch in an outstretched hand, barely illuminating their path with the slowly dimming sapphire light.

"Damn stick is about out," Henri mumbled under his breath.

Seamus smirked. "You know, this was not exactly what I had in mind when I decided to stay on the Pearl." Seamus hated the quiet, and would do about anything to get a conversation going. The nagging feeling of those Biters finding them drove their feet forwards, but the stifling silence was even more uncomfortable than the incessant heat of the volcano.

"Not what you had in mind?" Henri's short response was tainted with derision.

"I mean, come on," Seamus chuckled. "How was I supposed to know we'd end up in a volcano?"

Henri did not scoff, nor did he laugh, he did not even complain. Not a word nor sound came from the young man as we continued forward. There were only the dull, echoing footfalls that come from bare feet slapping against the glassy stone.

"Come on, Lightfoot," and the irony of the name was not lost on Seamus. "Don't be that way."

Henri stopped suddenly and let out a long, exasperated breath. "You know, Seamus, I don't know if I like you or hate you. You have been the biggest thorn in my side. Were it not for you, I'd be on some observation deck, helping chart stars or plotting courses." he stopped talking suddenly, coughed, as if something was caught in his throat, but then continued, his voice a little raspy. "But I wouldn't, would I?"

"What do you mean?" Seamus asked, dropping the levity he was trying to force.

"Damn it, Quic- Seamus!" Henri fumbled his words. He never fumbled his words. Henri let out a sharp breath and pressed on. "I didn't have... friends. I never had them, never was a people person. They don't make sense, too volatile, too unpredictable. Do you know what I like about maps? You can read them, understand them."

"Sounds real exciting."

"For once, can you not just listen and keep your mouth shut?" Henri snapped. "I am trying to thank you!"

Was that embarrassment in his voice?

Miracle of miracles, Seamus did keep his mouth shut.

"I am no good with people. I don't have friends... I didn't, anyways," Henri continued. "But, if we're going to die in here, and I believe there is little statistical chance that we won't, I want you to know that you have always been a good friend."

"I - uh - erm, well, thank you?" Seamus said, looking down at his feet, unable to even look at the back of his friend.

"I didn't mean for you to get stripes and the collar," Henri said suddenly. "Master Charlie wasn't supposed to beat you. I just, I didn't want to lose. I always lose. All this is my fault. Had I just... we might not even, well, we was already in trouble. I just..."

The lump that formed in Seamus' throat felt like it would burst his next in half. His eyes stung with tears. "Gods! Gallae, Mother of All! Henri, you don't think this is all your fault?"

Henri did not reply, which was answer enough. More than enough. By Fenron's Blade! Henri, kind, quiet, chubby Lightfoot thought this was his fault? How? Why?

"Gods..." Seamus swore again.

"I was up for transfer, papers signed and ready by Captain Atura'poha'alana... and so were you," Henri's voice utterly broke. "We were to be freed, deckhands no longer. But... but I wanted to win, just once. I wanted to beat you, to feel the satisfaction of winning, just once. I damned us to Halfak's pit."

He didn't know. How could he know? Seamus had earned his freedom twice over. Halfak burn it all. The only reason Seamus stayed on the Pearl of Red Duchess was to bed Snapdragon and to be with Henri. He loved them both, differently, but he did love them. He knew that now, more than anything.

"Henri," Seamus said slowly. "You know this is not your fault. You can't think that it is. And that was a hell of a trick, setting me up so that it looked like I was the one. Damned clever. I always forget that you're so much smarter than me."

Henri turned around slowly. His eyes, illuminated by the sapphire light of the Fragtorch, were red and puffy, and his cheeks were soaked with tears. His shoulders were slumped, but they were lifted ever so slightly. A slow smile spread across his face. "You did take the bait rather easily, like a striper to a flashing jig."

"Well, hold on, I wouldn't go that far..." Seamus protested, raising his hands in mock argument.

"It was a good win," Henri sniffed.

"It was a damn dirty trick," Seamus spat, but he could not hold the smile back from his cracked lips. "I am glad you did it. I am glad you won. I'd rather die here with you, doing something exciting than living a boring life in some master's workshop as an apprentice shoveling coal. No one was going to take me. I can't read great, can't plot stars or chart maps with choreography."

"It's cartography," Henri interjected, but then went silent as a mouse, realizing that he had just broken the conversation's flow.

"You're right," Seamus laugh. "As you normally are. Anyways, thank you, for being my friend."

Henri's smile broadened, his shoulders lifted, but just before he went to speak, the whole earth shook beneath their feet. A low, grinding, grumble belched forth from the earth, and the two were swiftly reminded that they were standing in an active volcano, or at least, over the rivers of lava that ran beneath this cavern.

"Shall we?" Seamus said sharply.

"Yep!" Henri answered as he whirled about and hurried down the winding tunnel.

The ribbed tunnels of onyx seemed to go on forever, winding ever downwards. The heat became suffocating, the dry, acrid fumes nearly unbreathable. Sulfur burned at the eyes and nose, but onwards Seamus and Henri delved, deeper and deeper into the volcano's heart.

When Seamus was just about to give up and cave into despair, the tunnel opened into a massive cavern before their very eyes. A river of lava flowed far beneath the ledge upon which they stood, looming over the red-hot magma, like the bow of a ship cutting through the waves. Two stone structures jutted up from the black floor, not formed by nature, but crafted by hands. Colossal iron rings were affixed to the pillars, rising head and shoulders over Seamus and Henri. Chains of iron hung from the rings, their ends dropping into the lava, red-hot, but intact.

On the far side of the cavern rose a secondary column of onyx stone, two matching pillars with identical rings and chains. What stood on the far side of that column stole Seamus's breath. Hewn into the walls of the cavern stood the palisades of a massive gate. Where doors surely must have once stood, a gaping hole had been blasted by some mystical force. Stone, now frozen in time, still seemed to drip, as if melted by a great heat.

The spectacle was magnificent, and though it stunned the two for several long moments, reality came crashing back upon them. Seamus tore his eyes away from the intricately carved structure and began to look about for some means to span the burning moat of lava.

"Lightfoot, you see anything?" Seamus asked. His voice was low and unnatural, rasping out as he choked on the noxious air.

"Hu? What?" Henri had clearly not come back to reality as swiftly as Seamus had.

"We have to get across. Whatever the Heart is, I bet my soul it's in there," said Seamus as he pointed to the blasted gates. "But I ain't about to take a dip in that pit to get across." and his eyes fell to the river of boiling earth and stone.

"Oh, right," Henri answered. He shook his head and rubbed at his eyelids, holding his cracked spectacles in his off-hand.

"There has to be a way across," Seamus muttered out loud as he searched about. He had not traveled this far, gone through this much, to be stopped so short of his goal. And to be quite honest with himself, he wanted that Heart too, now that some much had happened in order to get to this point. Perhaps with it, he could truly save Una'pahu and get the hell off this Halfak-blasted island.

"Look at this!" Henri exclaimed.

Seamus whirled about to see what had caused Henri's excitement. To his horror, his friend was gone. No one else stood atop the hot, black rock but he.

"Lightfoot? Henri? Where in Halfak's seventh level are you?"

"Pull your head out," Henri laughed.

Seamus looked down at the ground near the cavern's wall, from where the voice was coming, and spotted the top of Henri's head, poking up. Cut into the floor, hidden by some bewitchment or trickery, a set of steps led downwards.

"There is a crank and pully system down here, but it's too tight for more than one person." Henri proclaimed. "Halfak's fiery gates, it's red hot! I think I burnt my hand just looking at it!"

"What are you talking about?" Seamus thundered, his heart rate falling back down to a normal tempo.

"A second," Henri called back. He popped up again as if rising from the floor itself. "It's a tight fit down there, I can barely fit myself," Henri said as he crack his neck this way and that.

"Let me take a look," Seamus said, pushing past his friend and taking the steep steps down into the pit.

To Seamus' dismay, there was little dishonesty in Henri's words. The room, if one could call it that, was tiny. A small seat, carved from the very stone, and a large wheel, not dissimilar from the captain's wheel of a ship, were all that was in the room, that and a window so that one could observe the farside of the caver. From the low vantage, Seamus could see a series of chains and pulleys, and quickly surmised that they could be used to raise a drawbridge.

"A drawbridge!" cried Seamus. "It's a bloody

drawbridge."

Excitement overtook him and he reached out and grabbed the great wheel, and subsequently screamed out in pain.

"Everything alright down there?"

"You can't touch the blasted wheel! How in Halfak's blazes are we supposed to lift the bridge?" Seamus called back, sucking on the tips of his burnt finger.

"Bridge?" Henri called back, his head appearing quizzically through the narrow opening, gazing down at Seamus.

"It's a drawbridge - the chains and rings - it's a bloody bridge! But how are we supposed to get across?"

"Didn't the Spector give you some special gloves?" the levelness of the tone Henri used made Seamus chagrin.

Of course, just use the damn bloody gloves! Obviously! Why wouldn't I think of that?

Seamus pulled the gloves out of the makeshift rope belt that held his trousers up. They were soaked with sweat, the salty water dripping off the scales. They were large, far too large to fit comfortably, and very stiff. But they did the job. Seamus pulled at the wheel, only the top half visible, the bottom half dipped below the floor in a hollow that had been carved to fit the great wheel. The room was altogether too small and cramped.

Slowly, painstakingly so, the bridge began to rise out of the lava. Planks of steel glowed red-hot, but by some bewitchment, were whole. Seamus pulled and pulled, watching the bridge rise through the window, all the while listening to Henri hoot, gasp in amazement, and cheer at the spectacle, no doubt running through the myriad of ways such a contraption could have been constructed.

"Thanks, Spec!" Seamus said aloud, looking from the stone window at the drawbridge's glowing planks and down at the dragon-scale gloves.

"Hurry on up!" Henri called down from above. "We gotta figure a way across now. Looks hotter than Halfak's gates."

Seamus, excited to get out of the stifling, cramped space, released the wheel and turned to head up the steep, stone steps. As he climbed, a low rumble echoed throughout the massive chamber.

"Ah, burn it all!" Henri swore in exasperation.

When Seamus's head poked out, he saw the cause of both the sound and the swearing. The drawbridge was sinking slowly back into the magma trench. Turning swiftly, Seamus looked down in horror to see the massive wheel turning in the opposite direction in great, slow intervals.

Seamus rushed towards the wheel and took hold of it with both hands, straining against the hot steel. He braced a foot against the wall and pulled back with all his strength, halting the lowering bridge. Frantically, he looked from side to side for something to halt the backward turning.

There had to be a leaver or break to stop the mechanism from lowering.

On the floor, like the peddle of a peddle boat couples used to ride the canals of Gal, sat two steel pedals. Seamus's heart soared, and then immediately flatlined. The pedals were broken. He tried to jam a bit into where the wheel was, but it did not fit, falling into the molten abyss beneath.

No no no! We've not come this far, dealt with all this shit, for this! Not to fail here!

Seamus fumed, unable to think of anything they could use. The silver casing of the map was smaller than the break that had fallen through the floor, and the Fragtorch was too thin. Seamus did not want to be halfway across the moat when the bridge decided to sink into the magma.

"Quickfingers," Henri's voice broke Seamus's muddle thought-stream. It was cold and calculated, slow with hesitation, but somehow firm with resolve. "I'll hold it."

"What? What are you saying?" Seamus replied.

"I can hold it, you can go and get the Heart."

"Are you out of your mind? Seamus fired back.

"We can't wait," Henri replied. "Reylelan and her crew will be here soon. The Specter said the only way we make it off this island is with the Heart. And we don't get that by standing around he arguing."

"No!" Seamus blurted out. "you said it yourself, Reylelan could be here any second. I'm not leaving you here alone!"

"So we stay here and die together?" Henri asked,

his voice calm but pleading. "This way, we stand a chance. There is no other way."

Seamus did not answer, not immediately. He looked around the cramped room, searching for anything. Why on Gallae's name would they make a place like this? What was it for? Why had the Specter sent them? What were they going to do?

"Seamus, come on, we need to do this, now."

"But, what if-" Seamus choked.

"No but's, no time. We can use our vests to wrap your feet. You can make the run if you hurry. I'll wait here, listening for your call. I'll be fine," Henri said.

Seamus climbed out of the pit, silently. His face was dark and somber. He looked his friend in the eyes and extend his hand. In his clenched fingers glistened the stiletto. "I swear on Fenron's Blade, I'll kill them all if something happens to you, Lightfoot."

"I don't think Fenron gives a damn," Henri laughed coldly but took the knife nonetheless.

Seamus handed over the gloves next and then took off his vest.

"It's going to catch fire the moment I step onto those planks."

"Piss on'em," Henri said flatly.

"I guess," Seamus shrugged.

"No," Henri said, a little color flashing on his cheeks as he took off his vest, laying it by the other. "We'll piss on'em. Won't help for long, but the bridge is not far. If you get a running start, that should hold them over."

"Oh, that's nasty," Seamus groaned, and burst out laughing; the disgust and realization mixing like oil and water in his gut.

Hot piss mixed with dirt and leather squelched between Seamus's toes. He wanted to vomit. There was no time. Henri had already disappeared into the tiny wheel-room, well, big wheel, tiny room. Seamus rubbed at his temples. He needed to focus.

"Ready?" cried Henri.

"Gallae save me," Seamus hissed out under his breath. "Ready!"

"Up she goes!"

Slowly the steel chains clinked and clanked, gears strained, and the blazing bridge lifted from the moat of lava. Seamus stared at the bridge, eyes wide with terror. His mind screamed in protest. His gut clenched, and had he had any piss left in his bladder, he was sure it would have been trickling down his leg at that very moment.

"Holy mother on high!" Seamus bellowed as he rushed forward at full speed.

Like eggs dropped into boiling grease, the piss-soaked vested wrapped about Quickfinger's feet sizzled and popped as they slapped against the red-hot panels of steel. Steam curled around his ankles at first, but then swiftly turned to smoke. And then he was across. His throat burned. Seamus had screamed the whole distance. He now choked on fumes, spluttering and coughing.

"You make it?" Henri cried from the small room.

"What in Halfak's depths does it look like?" Seamus shot back.

"You prick!" Henri rebutted. "Get that damn Heart and let's get out of here."

Right!

Seamus turned and faced the intricately carved gate, hewn directly into the sheer wall of the cave. Upon closer inspection, details sprung to life. Thousands of tiny carvings decorated the surface. Depictions of short, thickly built men and women going about a myriad of different tasks were etched with an artisan's hand. There were also engravings of taller beings, who rode on strange ships with odd sails, that furled to the sides of their ships, not up into the air. What made it stranger, was that the waves upon which they sailed did not appear level with the seas, but almost looked set in the clouds. These tall creatures had large eyes and pointed ears. The sight gave Seamus the shivers.

"Oye! Get a move on it!" Screamed Lightfoot, his voice straining as he fought against the pull of the wheel.

The cry jolted Seamus out of his study of the directions on the wall, and he turned his attention to the gaping hole in the stone. Seamus had never seen anything like it. It almost looked like a cannon blast, but more consistent. As if a thousand shots from heavy naval guns had struck in perfect succession, over and over again, striking the exact same spot. The very stone was melted around the edges, not shattered. And upon the floor, metal and stone mixed in frozen, glassy pools.

What in Halfuk's seventh level could have done this?

Before fear could take further hold on his heart and mind, Seamus stepped forward through the gaping wound and into the darkness beyond.

Chapter 16: The Sword and the Stone

Seamus did not know what he expected to see as he stepped through the melted hole in the stone gate, but the sight that filled his unsuspecting eyes stole his breath away. A veil of shadow had hung over the hole, separating the moat and this place, but once he had passed through, both words and legs failed him. He tripped on a crack in the green-grey floor, which shimmered like the sea's surface at night, dazzling the mind.

Dozens of octagonal pillars rose from the floor and reached to the vaulted ceiling, whose domed structure was ribbed with bronze-plated beams. The ceiling itself was set with polished silver, maxing the entirety of the surface reflective. Hundreds of chandeliers hung from the ribbed ceil, though their gemstone settings had long grown dim.

Light, however, poured in from ventilation shafts, reflecting off of colossal oval mirrors that were set into what looked like the shields of towering edifices of men with great beards, tied and beaded. Seamus looked at one of those men and saw that the granite from wince he was carved was covered with deep veins of minerals, that sparkled and shone in the moon's white light.

But all of these, the mirrors, the statues, the ceiling, and the pillars were nothing compared to what lay at the far end of the hall. Seamus looked from the colossal pile of bones to the crack upon which he had stumbled and swore. It was no mere crack, but the impression of three massive talon-marks, and a great scaled foot.

A chill ran down Seamus's spine and the urge to turn and run through the hole in the wall and back to his friend nearly overtook him. But he steeled himself and pressed forward. Slowly he stepped towards the bones of what he could only describe as a dragon. The tail of the beast was nearly as long as one of the columns was high, the bones of which, at the tip, were as thick as his leg and only grew in diameter as they rose to the spine and hindlegs of the creature.

Seamus made his way around the side of the beast, noticing for the first time that its bones were not the only ones scattered about the hall. Nor were old bones the only things littering the floor. Gold, jewels, and gemstones were amassed in a heap under where the belly of the dragon would have been. And in the center of the pile stone a solitary gem whose facets blazed with firelight, and through whose middle jutted out a white-gold blade of ludicrous proportions.

"Ho-ly..." Seamus gasped, staring at the handle of the blade, which was nearly as long as his torso, and in whose crossguard, a white gemstone was set.

In the back of his mind, something told him to stay his hand. But Seamus had always had a problem reaching for things he knew he shouldn't. Besides, what harm could touching an old sword do?

Seamus wrapped his fingers around the white, leather-wrapped hilt of the great sword and heaved upwards with one hand, placing the other upon the massive, sparkling gemstone.

The world exploded with light.

Heat, unlike anything he had ever known before, consumed his mind and body. Light, far brighter than the sun at noonday seared his eyes. Pain. Screams. His left hand melted upon contact with the gemstone, his flesh dripping off the bone. Ecstasy, pure elation surged through his body, filling his veins with power. His mind fractured and the room, the bones, mirrors, and statues bled away from his vision. His eyes shattered as beams of white light flared through the sockets. And all vanished.

Seamus blinked.

He was floating in midair. He tried to focus, but everything was strange and distorted. He was somewhere purple... lots of purple. Everything looked geometric; there were lines of silver and gold streaking through the sky or at least what Seamus assumed was the sky. Thunder rolled across the distance, rattling Seamus' mind. He reached his hands up to clog his ears but froze suddenly as he saw what they had become.

He could see through them both, though they looked nothing alike. On the right, his hand, forearm, and up look like they had been formed of translucent crystal, and beneath its surface, veins of gold flowed. On the left, his arm, which he could have sworn had been melted, was reformed of scale-like pieces of a gemstone, whose surface was cracked. And within the fissures ran streams of red light, pumping out of sync to that of the golden veins. The imperfection wound up his left arm and spread over his chest, abdomen, and shoulder. He could feel its taint on his neck and up the side of his face.

Terror struck. He could not breathe. He could not think. He could nothing but float in the nothingness that surrounded him. Seamus was utterly helpless.

Rage! Burn! Tear! Feast!

The thunderous, grinding voice boomed

throughout the expanse. Seamus cast his eyes about to see the source of the sound. Hot wind whipped at his face as two massive wings beat in the distance. A beast sped towards him, winding and twisting as it descended.

I'll not let you have him!

The second voice, like the first, boomed out from the nothingness. However, this was not a terrible sound, though it shook Seamus to the core. It was a beautiful, powerful voice, filled with valor and hope. And it sounded strangely familiar.

Seamus twisted about, seeking the owner of the second voice, and found himself praying in earnest for someone to save him from the oncoming dragon. A dragon that was growing horrifically closer.

Feast! Flesh! Death!

Not this day, fell beast! Cried back the regal voice.

Seamus's golden heart missed a beat. *By Gallae's grace!*

Take not my mother's name in vain, mortal.

Shit... Seamus gasped.

Feast!

This was not happening.

The sky split as a bolt of white lightning arced towards Seamus. He flinched and closed his eyes, ready to be struck by the prong. But, just as the bolt was about to strike him, his crystalline hand thrust itself outwards, and he caught the bolt in his bare hand. It was not a bolt of lightning, but a great and terrible sword, whose blade was longer than he was tall. Who's hilt was wrapped in white leather and in whose cross guard was set a perfect gemstone of brilliant white.

The emerald dragon, whose talons were blacked spearheads and whose teeth were one hundred swords, belched a torrent of flame. The sky shook and rippled, heat-haze distorting Seamus's vision. He hefted the wide blade, grabbed it at its center, and blocked the torrent of red-yellow flame.

He is mine! The dragon roared, its voice deep and dark as the ocean, and just as mysterious.

You shall not have him, for we have bonded! Replied the second voice.

Seamus's head spun, and despite the fear and the fight, he felt as if he were about to vomit.

Freed! I will not be caged again!

I slew you in life, you shall not defeat me in death.

The dragon dove and Seamus found himself propelled forwards, greatsword held high over his head. Which, had he thought about it, would have been impossible. That blade was massive, there was no way he could lift it. Time sure was funny here, wasn't it?

The purple sky cracked. Thousands of fissures marring the geometric infinity, like a great spider web. And through the cracks, he could see the columns, he could see the bones of the dragon, and he could see himself.

He was, Seamus, knelt over the gemstone still, holding the sword and the jewel. He was screaming, white and red flames twisting about him like a hurricane. His skin was melting off of the left side of his body and his eyes blazed with white light.

The dragon crashed into him, jaws wide. The fractured sky mended and his focus was back on the fight. Or whatever this was.

I will burn the world!

I won't let you harm the mortals! Seamus cried back in defiance. No, not Seamus, that was Fenron doing the talking. Right? Wait...

Burn false god! And another torrent of flames leapt from the dragon's mouth.

Seamus took the blade, holding the hilt in both hands, and turned the flat towards the onslaught of fire. The blade soaked up the blaze and began to glow with a fervent zeal. With a battle cry, Fenron thrust the blade into the dragon's shoulder.

Seamus wailed in agony. The crystalline surface of his own shoulder burst and hot, red liquid poured from the wound. Both Fenron and the dragon stopped immediately.

No! The dragon cried out.

This is not possible...

"What in Halfak's pit is going on?" Seamus screamed, his left arm hanging limp at his side.

No! No! No! The dragon raged, circling and lashing about.

This was not supposed to happen. The voice that was Fenron's echoed in Seamus's mind, his own voice somehow warped slightly, more gravitas and bravado. *This should not have happened.*

Fused! We are fused! I can feel your weakness in my bones, mortal.

Oh, my father... what I have done? Fenron cried out.

In an instant, it became clear, terribly, horrifically, crystal clear. The dragon, the blade, the voices. It was all in Seamus's head. He knelt atop a pile of gold and silver, steam rising from his naked flesh, grasping in one hand a greatsword and in the other a gemstone, no large than a cannonball. He looked at the multi-faceted jewel and saw the red light pulsating, matching his own heartbeat. Seamus wanted to drop the accursed thing, but couldn't feel his fingers.

His heart leapt into his throat. Slowly, he scanned the hand that held the gemstone. The flesh had reknit itself, but it did not look like it had before. It was reddish-pink, as if sunburned, but instead of smooth skin with freckles and hair, small surfaces covered his skin like that of a lizard. Like that of a dragon. The burns wreathed his forearm, and as far as he could tell, as in the realm of purple, covered the sides of his face and neck and torso.

His breathing came slowly, rasping against his lungs. They too felt changed, burned. But the room, it was so vivid now. Everything was crystal clear. He could see every detail, the carvings, and the structures. He turned and looked at the wall on the other side. A dozen or so large, arching doorways met his view, with steps leading up and down. Seamus then noticed something strange. The heat was not present in this room, not as it had been outside.

The door was sealed with Iarathor Wards, as was all of Dhalnalk'Ra.

That was right; Seamus knew that. Of course, he did, the Iarathor were skilled craftsmen and workers of stone and the arcane arts. It was no surprise that humans had based parts of their folktales on them, calling them Dwarves. Funny creatures, humans. So filled with imagination and vigor.

Pain assaulted Seamus's mind and he stumbled once more, the colossal blade clattering to the floor as he did so. He vomited blood and bile.

Blood! Grumbled the voice of the dragon in the back of Seamus's head. A torrent of rage surged through his veins.

The sword! Take up the sword!

No! Freedom! Blood! Flame and death!

Seamus let out a violent roar. He felt his skin tear at his spine and shoulderblades. Wings of black flame unfurled behind him. The very blood beneath his flesh boiled as red filled his vision. The Heart in his left hand pulsed wildly, *Thump-thump! Thump-thump!*

The blade, pick up the blade.

The voice was so faint now Seamus could barely hear it. He could taste blood in the air. Human flesh. His stomach grumbled. But then there was a wrongness also, something rotten and putrid. An ancient enemy to his draconic kin. Seamus hissed and roared, the sounds feeling more natural than the act of speaking in a human tongue.

Whatever was causing that horrid smell was drawing closer. He could sense the presence of several hundred creatures progressing through the caverns. He could - *Iodaba!*

Your friend is in danger! Take up the sword and fight for his life!

"Henri!" with the call of his friend's name, focus and control came back to Seamus. He stretched out a taloned hand and took hold of the greatsword by the hilt. The dragon screamed against it in his mind, but he resisted.

As soon as his fingers wrapped around the blade, a jolt of energy overtook his limbs. The wings vanished, wisping away into nothingness. The talons retreated into his flesh and his hand became human once more. The red vision fell from his eyes and he saw as a human once more, though still far better.

Your friend! Go! Go now!

Seamus ran.

***

Una'pahu stumbled weakly through the blackened tunnels of the volcano, a rope about her neck and a sword at her back. The remaining Biter whom Reylelan bedded held the rope, and he had death in his black eyes. Una'pahu guessed he had not yet recovered from the loss of his lover; his and Reylelan's. Una'pahu didn't care. On the contrary, when the demon looked at her, she mustered all her strength and smirked. The blinding slap came so fast that she had not the time to flinch. The metallic taste of blood filled her mouth as his icy hand struck, followed closely by the throbbing pain from the strike.

"Keep your hands to yourself!" Reylelan hiss at the shirtless Biter.

"She taunts me, mistress," the rage was not well hidden from his perfect voice.

"That's Captain! I own you and you will obey!" Reylelan whirled around, her irises already gathering tendrils of Antilight.

The Biter flinched back from his master, but Una'pahu stood her ground. She was going to die. She knew that. She did not know why she was still alive right now, but death was certain. And she would not face it with a tremble in her spine or fear in her heart. She was a Ta'ala Gau, a Wakatiti, and she would not cower before this heartless bitch!

"You have steel in your heart," laughed Reylelan. "Let's see what good it will do you when I tear yours out and replace it with the dragon's."

Oh. That was why they were keeping her alive. And did she just say dragon? Dragons did not exist anymore...if ever they did. That being said, dragon or not, the idea of having her heart ripped out did not make her feel more confident. She felt a little of that 'hard steel' soften in her resolve.

At long last they reached the end of their journey, the tunnel opening into a massive open chamber; after being carried on the naked back of the tall Biter through the jungle as they all ran a breakneck speed, the slow creeping through the tunnels had been painful. Una'pahu did not know how much more her nerves could take. More than her feet. They were cut hundreds of times over.

Una'pahu gasped. The site was like something out of a nightmare. They stood atop an outcropping of stone that hovered over a river of molten stone, the red-hot magma sending waves of endless heat through the colossal cavern. Two pillars of stone formed the anchors of a drawbridge. The steel planks were coal-black, but she could see the heat-haze distorting the air around them. Across the drawbridge was an intricately crafted gatehouse, carved straight into the stone of the mountain of fire; beautiful, imposing, broken. A gaping hole was blasted into the face of the gatehouse.

"We're close, children," Reylelan proclaimed, not trying to hide the elation in her voice in the slightest. A cruel smile slid across her perfect lips. She pointed to a group of disgustingly malformed Biters, "You four, make sure the bridge is crossable. Go!"

"Ma'am!" they cried in unison, their voices eager to serve, but devoid of human feeling. They scrambled over to the drawbridge and began to cross, their bare feet slapping onto the steel.

"Hot!" Cried out one of the Biters in a low, grumbling whimper.

"Ouch!" bellowed another, whose foot had caught fire. It tore its leg free trying to move forward but then fell flat on its face. The sizzling sound of searing meat made Una'pahu's stomach turn. But she could not deny the ugly throe of joy she felt at seeing her captors suffer.

"Then they have made it yet," Reylelan chuckled to the tall Biter that held the rope, placing a hand on his chiseled chest, tracing a finger down to the black leathers around his waist.

Una'pahu wanted to be sick.

"Does it make you uncomfortable, child?" Reylelan sneered, casting those deep, beautiful, patronizing eyes at her.

Una'pahu could feel the demon's pull on her even now. Despite the hate and fear, a part of her yearned to please Reylelan. A part of her wanted her to love her. It was intoxicating, humiliating - it was infuriating. Una'pahu sank her teeth into her own tongue, grinding until she tasted hot blood once more.

Focus. Don't let her in your head. You're not dead yet. Not yet.

"Once I place the Heart in you, you'll be much more... malleable. I think I shall like our journey home, far more," Reylelan said, turning away from Una'pahu and her man slave. "Now, back to the task at hand."

"My lady," the tall Biter who held Una'pahu's leash. "I smell blood."

Reylelan spun around on her heel, all the levity and glee erased from her perfect, little face. "What did you just say?"

"Blood, my lady," he answered in monotone serenity.

The pirate captain stood still for a long moment, her hands extended, palms turned upwards. A gentle breeze began to emanate from her body, materializing out of nothingness. The amulet that had rested in her low-cut blouse lifted, seemingly of its own accord. Una'pahu felt a chill in the air, despite the heat of the volcano. Runic symbols formed around her palms, black ink rimmed with sinister maroon veins.

"Chain her up," Reylelan commanded. Her voice had changed, grown deeper and darker. Some of the beauty had leeched from her face, her jaw becoming longer and teeth sharper. Her irises had turned to slits and her blazing hair floated about her head, appearing like one of those paintings of an angle's crown of fire.

"Yes ma'am!" Intoned the tall Biter as he saluted his mistress. He jerked the cords that held Una'pahu, dragging her body towards the two stone pillars.

Una'pahu screamed. She could not help herself. Everything about this moment was a nightmare; the fire, the heat, the Biters and their undead captain, and now, she was to be chained for some demonic sacrifice. The screams just kept coming. She dropped to the ground and wept, but the tall Biter grabbed her by the head with too-long fingers and dragged her to the black pillars.

He ran a chain through one of the iron rings and then tied it tightly around her left wrist. With a harsh pull on the chain, Una'pahu's arm was thrust upwards, nearly pulling her arm out of the socket. He then moved to the second iron ring, unwrapping a second chain from his waist.

"Please!" Una'pahu begged, thrashing her feet against the ground.

"Do not fret, child," the Biter said hollowly. "Our mistress will make you anew, and you shall never know fear nor death. Rejoice in the day of your rebirth."

"Gallae, Mother of All, hear my cry!" Una'pahu prayed to the heavens as her right arm was wrenched upwards, blood spilling from torn flesh about her wrists.

"We found one of them!" an indistinct Biter proclaimed.

Una'pahu looked across the jagged protrusion and, to her horror, saw two Biters dragging a bloodied, shirtless, gaunt Lightfoot towards Reylelan. And she stared at him with haunting, hungry eyes.

"I needed this," she smirked, running a black nail across his cheek. Una'pahu saw her friend flinch as the demon did so. "You shall-"

Reylelan's words stopped short. The sound of cogs, wheels, and chains moving filled the room. Una'pahu craned her neck to see the drawbridge lowering slowly into the lake of molten rock.

Reylelan screeched, then struck Henri across his face with an open hand, knocking the poor boy to the ground. "What have you done?"

All eyes were turned on Henri as he hefted himself onto his knees with both hands, shaking and spitting blood.

"Wait, didn't you have a little friend?" Reylelan asked, leering over her prey.

***

Henri met the demon pirate's eyes, hatred boiling beneath his flesh. His body trembled with rage, though he hoped that those around him thought it was a shiver of fear and pain. He was going to die, but he did not care. He would redeem himself. He would save his friends, somehow.

A thunderous roar filled the chamber, shaking the very ground. Suddenly, Henri found himself no longer the center of attention. And when he looked across the chasm, he understood why.

A figure emerged from the blasted hole in the stone-carved gatehouse. It was a tall, broad, humanoid creature, maned with crimson hair. It carried in its right hand a sword too large for any mortal to wield, white and silver, in whose cross guard was set a brilliant diamond. In its left hand, which was melted, scaled, and grotesque, it held a gemstone. One of its eyes blazed with white light, while the opposite pupil was slit like that of a poisonous snake.

The creature turned its unnatural eyes upon the conclave of Biters and let out a second, thunderous roar. It threw the blade it held, sending the massive weapon end over end, until in crashed into the two Biters that held - had held - Henri. Their bodies were cleaved in twine, like a hot knife through butter. The greatsword sliced into the wall behind them, driving itself nearly to the cross guard into the stone.

Reylelan screamed in defiance at the beast. She grabbed at the amulet about her neck, breaking that chain that held it, and shattered the silver in her hand. With a deep breath, she inhaled the flickering tendrils of black Antilight that emanated from the broken necklace.

Henri saw his moment. No longer bound, no longer watched, he slid the stiletto from his belt and leaped that the demon, slamming the slender blade to its hilt between her shoulder blades.

***

The sword! Get the sword! You must hold the sword!

Hate! Burn! Consume!

Seamus's mind fractured again. He tried his best to focus, to take in what was happening, but those voices in his mind never stopped. Wincing in pain, he forced himself to see his surroundings. Dozens of Biters swarmed about the adjacent outcropping of stone, drawing cutlasses, pistols, and sabers. Others must have found the small wheelhouse, as the drawbridge was slowly raising once more.

"Snapdragon!" Seamus bellowed. Hearing his own, cracked voice he took a step back in confusion. *What have I become?*

Anger burned away his thoughts, consuming

his mind. Una'pahu was chained up, stripped to her shift, and bleeding. Henri was - gods be damned. Henri had just assaulted the bloody Captain of the Black Sister.

We can destroy them! The dragon's cruel voice intoned in his mind. *Let me burn them!*

You must not give in. Get to my sword. We can still save your friends.

They are perished. We can avenge!

"Shut up!" Seamus roared. He felt the flesh tear at his shoulder blades. He could feel the flames and darkness flow from his back, forming wings of death. He ran to the edge and leapt.

The hot air whipped at his face, pulling at the hair on his head. But it felt good, it felt right. The heat was his alley, the flames, his friends. He landed with a resounding *thud!* The earth beneath his taloned feet cracked, and with the swing of his left hand, gemstone still held fast, he cracked the skulls of three Biters. They fell lifeless before him.

Reylelan was screaming, one hand reaching towards the middle of her back, the other grasping Henri's neck. Biters rushed towards Seamus, not fearing death nor pain, their only desire was the will of their mistress.

The pirate captain wrenched the stiletto free from her back, a spray of black blood dripping from its sharp edge. She leaned down, forcing Henri's back into the hot stone, and thrust the knife at his heart with a smile on her bloody lips.

Seamus flew.

Fenron vs The Wyrm of Duka'unka'falla

Chapter 17: Fight

Seamus roared savagely as his powerful legs launched him forwards as the two, massive wings at his back beat wildly, propelling him directly into Reylelan. It felt like he had flown directly into a solid pillar of marble. His shoulder cracked and his eyes filled with tears instantaneously. But he was not the only one hurt, not this time.

Reylelan was flung from her place, striking the wall right by where the greatsword protruded.

When she lifted her head, black antilight leaked from her eyes and mouth, running like spilled ink onto her pale flesh. The pirate queen had two small, leather bags at her curvaceous hips, that had become tangled and twisted in the strike. With frustration, she unbuckled the belt and let the two bags fall to the floor, spilling their contents. She then drew a cutlass from its sheath, the sound of glass shattering reverberating through the room as the tainted blade hissed forth.

"I'll take that," Reylelan snarled, pointing the squared end of her blade at Seamus's left hand, where the Heart was still locked in his taloned fingers.

"Come and take it!" Seamus echoed in defiance, his voice broken and raspy, a bit of the dragon he heard in his head slithering forth of his tongue.

"I've killed thousands, you think you scare me? I am of the Dorr A'Gadah, chosen by the Great and Terrible Khadais, called to usher in the Dispensation of Darkness!" Reylelan spat.

The wounds on her body were knitting themselves together as she spoke. Seamus, or rather, Fenron, recalled how Iodaba's dark Touch could health those who performed blood rites. A sickening sensation churned in his guts, and then the realization that Una'pahu was tressed up, like a lamb for the slaughter.

The sword! You need the sword! Call the sword! Let me bite! Rend! Tear!

Seamus, you need the sword. No Ethrean material can harm a Morrean. They have sworn blood oaths and made corrupt pacts with the Fallen Ones. We must eradicate her.

Eradicate? The dragon fumbled the word on its forked tongue. A hot pleasure filled its thoughts, *I like that word!*

Reylelan surged forwards, moving faster than sight. And yet, somehow, Seamus was able to track her motions. It looked almost as if she were diving through water, misting ripples of Iodaba distorting the air as she moved from place to place.

Seamus sprang forward, ripping the white sword from the wall. Instantaneously, the dragon within tamed, the wings puffed away, and clarity overtook him once more. Yet, in the dark recesses of his mind, he heard the beast grumble, *eradicate!*

"By Gallae's Grace, is that you, Seamus?"

Seamus whirled around, looking for the source of the voice, all while a dozen or so Morreans rushed towards him, spewing out of the tunnel's opening onto the spit of rock. He quickly spotted the source of the voice. On the ground, not two paces away, Henri lay helpless. Seamus leaped forward, swinging the massive sword with ease; the blade felt lighter than air, and when it met the boney flesh of the Morreans, it sang with savage glee. It cut through them, disemboweling some and shattering others.

These are no normal Morreans. They're dead.

Seamus tried his best to shut out the proud, and yet somewhat confused, the voice of Fenron as he carved his way through an endless sea of bodies. The smell in the chamber was horrific. Dead, rotten flesh sizzled as he reared onto one leg and kicked two of the pale demons over the edge of the cliff. Others laid about him, guts and black blood oozing out, making the ground slick with gore. It was not a pleasant place to be.

"Another move and she dies!" Screamed Reylelan.

Seamus turned slowly, stepping carefully over the body of Henri and facing Reylelan. The demon pirate stood just off to the side of Una'pahu; the tall, shirtless Biter was stationed behind Una'pahu with a bone-handled knife pressed harshly against her neck. A trickle of blood dripped from where the razored edge of the blade had nicked her flesh. Hate welled within, and he could feel the dragon writhing in his mind, begging to be freed, begging to kill.

Do not act in haste, Fenron's regal voice implored. *Think of your friends.*

We can burn them all to ash and cinder!

"Is this what you want?" Seamus screamed in defiance to the voices in his head, struggling to maintain his hold on reality as he knew it. He extended his left hand, the crystal pulsating fiery light in his fingertips.

"A trade?" asked Reylelan, her voice steadily leveling. The ink-black veins that ran the length of her cutlass seemed to undulate upon the surface of the bright steel. She pointed the blade towards Seamus; all eyes fell on him, silent and foreboding. "You give us the Heart and walk away, and I shall let you take your friend there." the tip of the blade slowly dipped downward, pointing towards Henri.

"She comes with me," growled Seamus, pointing his chin towards Una'pahu.

"Ha!" Reylelan blurted out. "You are in no position to negotiate."

"You would not be speaking if that we true," Seamus snapped back, his eager tongue moving faster than he could control. *Damnit, Seamus! We're trying to save our friends here, not win a war of words!*

"The girl stays with me, she is mine now." Passion and venom tainted the words that slithered out of Reylelan's mouth.

Seamus could feel the effects of her pull on him, but it was changed now, not nearly as strong as it had been before. He moved one foot back, stepping slowly to prepare himself to launch into an attack. When he did so, he felt something strange beneath his foot. The soft touch of leather and then the cold flow of water, rushing from a burst skin soaked the ground. A long, cylindrical rod of metal rolled, clinking lowly on the stone. He could not afford to look down, but he did not miss the look in Una'pahu's eyes as his foot revealed the object to her.

A plan, howbeit far stretched, formed in his mind. A thousand little moments flashed in his mind's eye as he sorted out the next few moments in a single instance.

"Now, give me the Heart and leave," Reylelan

snarled. "I shall command my children that no harm shall come upon you. Oh, and drop that blade. I don't want you getting any ideas."

Seamus did not listen to what the demon was spouting off now, his mind had used those precious moments to lock in the plan of action. Slowly, Seamus extended his left hand and began to lower himself into a crouch, shifting his right arm back, so that the greatsword's tip scrapped across the ground behind him. He placed the Heart upon the ground gingerly, having to mentally force his claw-like fingers to release the sphere.

"Drop the sword," commanded Reylelan. The pitch of her voice was upturned, and Seamus could see the hunger in her eyes, the elation of anticipation. Her tongue slid across perfect teeth in an unsettling way.

"As you wish," Seamus answered, letting the blade fall from his hand.

Reylelan stepped cautiously forward, the tip of her blade pointing at Seamus's face as she walked. Her smile grew across her face, the beauty giving way to a horrific, rictus smile. Her doe-eyes became infernal pits of desire and flame. Seamus could not help but feel a jolt of terror rush down his spine, but he did not move a muscle.

Grinning triumphantly, Reylelan plucked the Heart from the ground. For a long moment, everything was silent and still as the demon gazed into the multi-faceted face of the gemstone. The light danced off of her pale, marble skin, making her already perfect body glisten.

"Kill them." the command came with such nonchalance that Seamus almost missed it.

"You said-" Seamus started.

"Cut out her heart!" Reylelan commanded, turning away from Seamus, strutting towards Una'pahu.

"Catch!" Seamus bellowed, flinging the silver rod that he had seen Snapdragon holding as she commanded the very waves of the sea, and then diving into Reylelan's hard figure.

The rod, which Seamus had snatched from the ground as he had knelt down, dropping his own sword, twirled through the air and landed directly in Una'pahu's open hand as if it had been drawn to her grasp by magic. Una'pahu's green irises flashed with fury.

***

Una'pahu's being felt as if it were about to burst with the surge of energy that now coursed through her veins, threatening to consume her. She had gone from scared and helpless to alive with power and rage. Her palm burned as something seared into her flesh. In her mind, she heard a phrase, *Ada'aha El-dached!*

Without realizing it, she spoke the words back, causing the Biter behind her to shift at the unnatural words. His hands went slack; what she had said scared him. The bone-handled knife fell away from her neck.

With a twitch of her wrist, the water that was

leaking from the burst skin formed into a liquid lance and shot across the short distance, passing through her own body and impaling the Biter that stood befuddled behind her. He screamed in pain as he was flung outwardly. And when his body hit the river of magma, a plum of black smoke burst forth as his body popped like grease on a hot pan.

Una'pahu willed the water to cut the chains at her wrists, the liquid forming into blades that sliced through the metal with ease. Una'pahu was free once more, and she would never be chained again.

***

"Enough!" Screamed Reylelan, slamming her elbow into Seamus's chin, launching him off her back. She rose to her feet in a fury, looked around the precipice, and shrieked, "I am a god, and you will bow before me!"

"I see no god here," Seamus growled in defiance while he extended his right hand. The great sword answered its master's mental call. "Other than me!"

"You-... you arrogant, thoughtless, useless meat-sack!" Railed Reylelan furiously.

Seamus' eyebrows lifted at the insult. He had been called many things in his life, but never meat-sack. *Whatever floats her boat, I guess?*

"You are nothing! I will hack off your arms and legs, I will slice off your eyelids, and I will make you watch as I carve out her heart!" Reylelan roared.

Reylelan's screams of rage were cut short when she

turned her head to point at Una'pahu, her boiling anger was turned to surprise. She had apparently not seen Una'pahu gut her first mate, nor had she seen her use her Ta'ala Gau abilities to free her from her chains. The surprise depended as she saw the three orbs of water swirling in the air as Una'pahu began the Dance of the Waves.

Reylelan's head snapped back to Seamus, who stood holding the white blade, Fenron's Lost Blade; lost no longer. She then looked down at her hand, at the gemstone she clutched, and then back out at those around her. A malicious smile spread across her face.

"Kill them!"

The sound of glass shattering filled the air and Reylelan puffed out of sight. Seamus whirled around, searching for any sign of the demon witch. A second echo of shattering glass filled the air, and at the mouth of the tunnel, Reylelan materialize, behind the bulk of the remaining Biters.

"Kill them all," she snarled with finality. She then walked away, sheathing her cutlass, the Heart held proudly in her hand.

All at once, dozens of Biters began to flood into the chamber through the tunnels, hemming Seamus in and allowing Reylelan to stroll away without a care in the world. There was nothing he could do to stop her.

Anger and frustration threatened to overtake him, and though faint, he could still feel the dragon within. The desire to drop the sword and give in to the beast was palpable. But when he looked out once more, he saw something more important than the Captain of the Black Sister, more important than the fight or the Heart. Seamus saw Lightfoot - his friend - had picked himself up and retrieved the stiletto from the ground; he held it in a fighter's stance, the dragon-skin gloves still protecting his hands. Seamus saw Snapdragon - his lover - moving with a grace and a ferocity that both scared and, if he was being honest with himself, slightly aroused him.

Fight today, find tomorrow. Fenron's voice echoed in his mind.

Let us burn with fire and rend with tooth and claw.

Well, it seems like we're in agreement? Seamus mused in his own mind.

Allow me to show you the power of the Ellitheor!

The massive white blade burst into flame. Seamus felt a surge of power ripple through his flesh. The world snapped into focus, as if he had lived his whole life in a dream and he only now experienced lucidity. The Morreans we rushing forward, their disproportionate, boney, bodies eager to meet their end. Seamus Arc'Fenron would grant them this last pleasure.

***

Reylelan breached the cave, the distant cries of death dimming as exited the dragon's maw. The sky was shifting. Dawn's light was swiftly creeping forth. She hissed in frustration. She had the Heart though, which was the main reason why she had been sent. The Khadais would be most grateful for her service. She could almost hear the ingratiating tones as he lauded her with praise.

A smile tugged at her lips as she thought of the rage and envy that would be shared by the other Dorr A'Gadah, especially that prick, Edous. She would revel in her victory, she would laud this over them for all eternity. Not getting the Ta'ala Gau was unfortunate, for reasons that she kept to herself; but she would find another. They were out there. One was awake, and this one did not even know what she was.

There was time. There was always time.

***

Ichor, limbs, and entrails bestrew the ground. It had been wanton suicide, what these Morreans had done - no, the Biters; they were Biters. Seamus had to get control of his mind. It was filled with thoughts, memories, and words that were not his own, some of which weren't even human. Seamus externally looked no better than he felt internally. He was soaked with black-grey blood of the Biters that laid about his feet, hewn and hacked to pieces. Seamus had to give Fenron this, the god knew how to butcher.

"Quickie," Snapdragon called out through gasps of air. She had been no less than majestic in the fight, moving about like a viper, striking with her strange Ta'ala Gau abilities, commanding the water and bending it to her will. "Are you in there?" Her voice sounded shaken, afraid even.

"What do you mean?" Seamus asked, turning his head to face her.

The expression on Una'pahu's face did not belie the tone of her voice. She stared at him as if he were a monster. Liquid ice spread throughout his body, chilling him to the bone despite the heat of the chamber.

"Well, for starters, you're taller," Henri answered in one of his false-jovial tones. Seamus could hear the pain and worry in his friend's voice. It did not help. Henri then cracked a grin, "And naked. Good on ya, buddy."

Seamus looked down. He was in fact naked. "By Gallae's breath!"

Guard your tongue!

These voices in his head, always arguing, always commenting, were going to get very old, and quick. Seamus brought his left hand up to wipe the weariness and stress from his face. He froze, actually examining his hand for the first time.

The sick had been burned away. A faint memory of some fleeting dream tugged at his mind. He thought, for a moment, he had been enveloped in flame and flew with the gods in some strange realm of purple skies.

"How..." Seamus started, but then the words were choked off. He sighed. "How bad is it?"

"Seamus," Una'pahu said quickly, stretching her

hand out, but then halting suddenly as he turned his gaze on her. She looked worried.

"We don't have time to worry about looks," said Henri, drawing upon some newfound resolve.

Seamus turned his gaze on Henri and winced. His friend was caked in mud and blood, not all of it black. Deep gashes marred his arms, and chest, with an especially nasty one carved into his brow; the meat of his forehead flopped over slightly revealing the bone beneath. He still wore the dragon-skin gloves and a certain hardness was itched into his demeanor. Seamus was not the only one who was changed this day, and that hurt his soul to its core.

"We're alive, and that is what matters," Snapdragon stated boldly, turning both boys' attention from one another. Despite the weeks of torture, Una'pahu's authoritative glare was unphased, and it demanded respect. She truly was a Wakatiti. "We need to go. I assume one of you has a plan?"

"Ya," Henri said, gathering his facilities. "We got to get the Heart to the Specter, he said he could use it to get us off the Island."

"Except we don't have it," Seamus groaned. "Reylelan took it."

"That that bloody witch! I mean to place her head on a pike outside my mother's house!" Una'pahu swore.

For some reason, Una'pahu's unbridled rage and ferocity were comforting to Seamus. He felt oddly safe now that she was back; as if some small part of the universe had been made right. He wanted to take her up in his arms. He wanted to hold her, kiss her, to breathe her in and all to be silent. But he was no longer himself. He was scarred and changed; some grotesque monster with the souls of a warring dragon and a god consuming his mind.

"Right," Henri said, clearing his throat. "Well, I still believe he is our best hope off this island."

"Well, let's hope your friend can make something out of what he has," Una'pahu stated, squaring her shoulders to the task.

"One moment," said Seamus as he stalked over to a particularly large Biter. He drove the tip of the great sword into the earth and lifted the creature with uncanny ease; an unsettled feat that he did not have the time to think about right now. He removed the demon's boots and then stripped it of its trousers. He pulled the pants up oddly muscular legs, noting that the burns stopped mid-abdomen and did not descend to his groin or thighs. *Be thankful for the little things*. He scoffed to himself. He turned and faced his friends, straightening the belt and retrieving the blade. "Onward then?"

"There might be more trouble on the way," Henri said, stretching at his thick beard. "Reylelan doesn't strike me as one to leave loose ends undone."

"I'll deal with that," Seamus answered darkly, resting the flat of the massive blade on a bare, brawny shoulder.

"It's settled then?" Una'pahu's question was not so

much a question as it was a statement. She turned away from her two friends and walked stalwartly through the tunnels, not an ounce of fear to be seen.

***

Jacques lay on the small boat staring up at the volcano, all the while focusing on breathing. Every breath drawn was short and painful; every exhalation was excruciating. He had laid on the beach, head propped up on his rolled cloak through the heat of the day and into the dark of the night. He had laid and done nothing while the greatest discovery in his lifetime, perhaps three hundred lifetimes, was taking place.

Something in his bag began to pulsate with a faint blue light.

Jacques placed the golden mask back over his sweat-soaked face and reached for the source of the light. It took him a moment to find the convex glass, whose silver rim was set with four gemstones that glowed softly with Aetora's eternal light. The lens was slightly smaller than the palm of his hand, and at the base of the rim, there was a small indention. In the center of this, a tiny needle was set.

Jacques removed his glove and placed his thumb on the tip and pressed firmly. Blood welled in the indention as the tip of his finger began to whiten. He felt that strange pressure in his chest he always felt when Aetora pulled at his soul. A sound like rushing water filled his ears as the glass began to swirl, the gemstones flickering growing faster and faster with every breath.

Suddenly an image appeared in the glass. A figure, masked in golden and adorned in chains and jewels materialized out of the misty-blue light of the apparatus. It was not a perfect image, but Jacques knew immediately the head of the secret order of the Asterivae.

"Illuminated One, I answer your call," Jacques proffered humbly.

"My Right Hand, my sword and my strength," came a faint, distorted reply. The Asterivae had not yet been able to perfect the Communicae Glass, but they were getting closer and closer. "Report."

"We have found, Duka'unka'falla," Jacques answered.

"You do not sound well, old friend," the answer came after a long moment of silence.

"I shall live, Illuminated One. I have survived worse," Jacques answered truthfully. The very hand he held the Communicae Glass with was mettle, as was his leg. Both were lost in the Calun Wars; both were replaced by the cunning of the Asterivae.

"And the Heart?"

"I shall have it soon," Jacques answered, though he could not totally conceal the doubt in his voice.

"Has something gone wrong?"

"Illuminated One," Jacques' answer came slowly, methodically. He was still not certain himself, but he needed to report on his findings. “I believe those who were called in ancient times Dorr A’Gadah have once again risen from their places of shadow and secrecy.”

“This is a dark thing,” came the answer after several more long moments of silence. “Have you any proof of this claim?”

“One who calls herself Reylelan, known as Captain of the Black Sister, she can Touch Iodaba. She has risen herself an army, tainted by the unholy antilight. They besieged the ship on which I had set sail, sinking her to the depths and taking me hostage. I managed to escape but took a round to the body. But that is not all. Master, I may have found one of the Sleeping.” Jacques could barely contain the excitement in his tone. “Master, I found one who can tap the Source of a Tel’un Aund. And, it was not Aetora’s light, but Ria’Elahm.”

Silence.

“Can you hear me, Master?” Jacques asked, pressing his thumb even harder upon the point.

The reply came swiftly, the Illuminated One’s voice deep in contemplation, but the excitement was unmistakable. “Do you realize what this means?”

“Master, the time is come at last!” Jacques answered in excitement.

“You must bring her at once. This command supersedes all others. Do whatever it takes, but bring me that girl and the Tel’un Aund.” The

Illuminated One instructed. "The world is about to change. There are forces at play now that have slumbered for centuries. When you return to the Asterivae, there is much to discuss. It suffices me to say this though, that I believe there is a Sleeping One here, in the very heart of Ordiatea, along with something else entirely... someone who could change the very fabric of reality as we know it."

"Your word is my command, Illuminated One!" Jacques answered with excitement. As soon as he lifted his thumb from the point, the image inside of the convex glass misted away.

A renewed sense of vigor entered Jacques's broken body. His mind was ablaze with ideas, with hope. He stood and looked upon the brilliant orange of the rising sun just peeking out over the horizon. There was hope, there was purpose. He had a plan and he knew what he needed to do. Now, all that he needed was for those boys to get back with the Heart.

Something stirred among the trees; it was the sound of a small group approaching rapidly. *They've made it back! Thank the stars*. Jacques rose, attempting to hastily tuck the silvery Communicae away.

***

Seamus lead the way, much to Una'pahu's protests, but she just did not know the way to the Specter, and they needed to get to him as quickly as possible. They were near the beach, only a few feet away. The thick jungle had thinned to tall palms and underbrush.

"Quickfingers." the cry caused Seamus to stop dead in his tracks. He turned about quickly to find Henri leaning against a tree, breathing raggedly.

"Come on, Lightfoot, you can make it." Seamus's breath was even and steady, despite the near run from the volcano.

His friend looked far from alright. He had wrapped a makeshift bandage around his head after Una'pahu had used her Ta'ala Gau abilities and that strange, silver rod, to cleanse the wound. Despite that, he looked ill, his face was pale and his hand trembling.

"We're at least a mile from shore. Run ahead, let him know we're coming," Henri wheezed. "I can show Snapdragon the way. I just can't run any further."

Seamus looked from his friend to Una'pahu. She too looked fatigued, though her body was not marred with the many cuts and bruises that Lightfoot bore. Seamus's face tightened and his mouth soured. He did not want to leave his friends behind him. But the sun was swiftly rising. He knew the Biters could not stand the light, though he was uncertain in Reylelan would share the same disdain.

"Seamus, look at me," Henri pressed. "We need to get off this island. Perhaps you can help devise a way once you get to him and we'll be ready to go when Una'pahu and I arrive."

Seamus chewed on the words for a few moments, batting away the grumbling rage of the dragon and the haughty proclamations of the god within. Fenron wanted to seek out Reylelan and deliver righteous justice. The dragon simply wanted to burn and feast. Both needed to be silent so Seamus could think.

"Fine," Seamus conceded at long last. "I will go ahead. Are you sure you remember the way?"

"I am the map guy," Henri said with a narrowing of his eyes and a half-hearted scoff. "Directions are my thing."

"Fine, fine!" Seamus snapped. "I'll go. But I am not happy about it."

"I don't give a damn if you're happy or not," Henri scoffed bitterly. "I just want off this gods-forsaken island."

I was not forsaken! I was trapped here because of this beast!

I shall rend your flesh from your bones!

"Enough! Once I get that bloody heart back and get home we are going to sort all this out and I am getting you both removed from my head!" Seamus screamed in his mind. *There is a way to get you out, right?*

No answer.

So now you go silent? Seamus fumed. *Fine! Be that way, but stay out of my way.*

"I'll see you on the beach." Una'pahu looked Seamus in the face, and he could not unsee the pity in her eyes. He was a monster.

"Until then," Seamus said with a wink of his

draconic eye, trying to play off the hurt he felt. "Upwards!"

Plums of flame and smoke burst from Seamus's back as flesh tore and great wings emerged from his back. Hot wind bellowed outwards as his wings thrummed, lifting him high above the tree line. Seamus flew towards the beach, to the place where their boat had washed upon, what seemed like a lifetime ago.

Seamus landed in a maelstrom of wind, sand, and flame. He hurried to the boat, the sand hot on his bare feet as he ran. To his horror, the small boat was absolutely empty. Where their hope of salvation, the Specter, had once sat, there was only a stain of blood. Wildly, Seamus searched the ground. Three sets of prints littered the sandy shore. One set, in particular, caught his eye. A small print with a raised heel; the boot of Reylelan. Seamus's mind raced as his guts seemed to drop.

How had she found him? What were they going to do? How could they escape?

No no no! This can't be happening! First Snapdragon, then the Heart, and now this?

Seamus fell to his knees, despair sinking her dark claws into his will and ripping the fragile remnants to shreds. He fell to the sand, dropping the blade beside him and gave way to the overwhelming desire to weep.

Something cold and smooth met the tips of his fingers, foreign to the hot sand of the beach. Seamus thrust his hands forwards, taking hold of an odd bit of silver in the form of a polished, oval mirror. It had a series of gemstones around the rim of the device, one of which was cracked, allowing a tiny tendril of light to leak from within into the air. The mirror's surface, like the pulsating gemstone, looked like the web of a silk-spider, fractures covering the plane.

"Mh!" grunted Seamus. Something sharp pricked his finger. A droplet of blood-soaked a small indentation at the bottom of the mirror.

Seamus blinked in surprise as an image crackled over the fractured mirror, lasting only the briefest of moments. A golden mask, much like the one that the Specter wore, only more decorative appeared. And though Seamus could not make out any aspects of the face behind the mask, the startled twitch of the head let him know that somehow, through this strange mirror, he the masked individual could see him.

The image vanished as quickly as it had appeared. Seamus pressed his thumb into the point where he had accidentally drawn blood moments before. Nothing happened. He let out a cry of distress, launching himself into the air, propelled upwards by the beating of the great wings of smoke and flame. He gazed outwards, scanning the darkening horizon. Nothing.

He and his friends were stranded, utterly alone with no hope of escape.

Furious at the cruelty of fate, Seamus let himself fall to the beach once more. Smoke swirled about him as the wings vanished. He took hold of the hilt of the massive sword. A chill ran up his arm as a calm clarity rushed through his mind. He could hear two sets of footfalls making their way through the forest towards the beach - Henri and Una'pahu.

I can be strong for them, Seamus steeled himself, rising from the sand, using the blade to support himself. *I can find a way off this cursed rock. I have to. I will.*

The End of Azure Tides

This story will continue in *Chains of a Broken God, Book Two of the Last Son of the Feromage Saga*

ABOUT THE AUTHOR

David Andrew Trotter was born in Ozark, AR to Jolene and Garry Trotter. He lived out his youth in that same small town, learning to love reading and exploring the wilds of his imagination. As he grew, his love of all things fantastic flourished. Eventually, he met - and quiet a long time later - married the love of his life, Heather Trotter. They share their home with their three children, Oliver, Lily, and Theodore and one pup, Tripp. David began writing fantasy as a means of escapism, after going through a very dark time in his life. This story, and all those that are attached to the Last Son of the Feromage Saga are attributed to these factors. David sincerely hopes you enjoy this instalment and bids you well as you set sail upon *Azure Tides*.

Glossary Of Terms, People, and Places

Characters of Note:

Captain Atura

High Captain of the Galacian vessel, *The Pearl of Red Duchess,* and tutor to Una'puha. High Captain Atura'poha'alana is of the upper crest of Galacain society called, Wakatiti. She is bold, firm, and unwavering. She runs a tight ship and leads with exactness.

Captain Reylelan Trallae

One of Diabhail's Dorr A'Gadah – Burning Hand – Reylelan is an extremely powerful vampiric enchantress. She has the ability to Turn mortals into mindless servants. Those who turn willingly retain the beautiful, vampiresque forms. Those who fight become mindless drone whose flesh barely holds to their bones.

Fenron

Eldest son of Gallae and Ordan, Fenron was a god in his own right, being worshipped by many. He was know for slaying Uuradan, the Great Dragon. He swore vengeance upon the wyrms of Ethrea, pledging to eradicate them from the world. It was said he fought the last dragons upon the forgotten shores of the accursed island, Duka'unka'falla.

Master Charlie

Owner of the title, 'Master o'Decks', Charlie is a hard man who struggles to find the line between care and abuse. He is strong and proud, but often overextends his hand when it comes to punishment.

Henri Sjo

Henri, also known as 'Lightfoot', was a boy when he was taken into the service of the Galacian Shipping Guild. Being a Msa'oo - Serving Man – Henri was forced into labor upon the *Pearl of Red Duchess*. It was upon her deck that he met the infamous Seamus Pearson, starting a fast friendship steeped in plots, petty theft, and shenanigans that would find them both collared and whipped more than once.

Jacques Lassourreille

Spector, Hand of the Illuminated, and many other names does this mysterious man go by. But who is he really? And more importantly, what does he want with the Heart?

Seamus Pearson

Born on the streets of Calun, sold into indentured servitude by his parents to Galacian merchants, and eventually finding himself mixed up in a heist-gone-wrong under Belfor the Boss, Seamus is an absolute mess of a human. His freckled face and wild red hair - however foreign they appear to the Galacian's – caught the eye of the daughter of a noble Wakatiti family. His quick whit and quicker hands gained him the alias 'Quickfingers'. His story only begins with what he thought was the end.

Una'pahu

Daughter of one of the most prestigious families in all the Matriarchy of Galacia, Una'pahu Mue'Mora has been blessed by her ancestors with the unique ability known as Ta'ala Gau – Wave Guiding. She is sent by her mother to be trained under the ridged instruction of High Captain Atura'poha'alana. Una'pahu's body, like the High Captain, is adorned with tribal tattoos, but unlike the High Captain, her eyes are bright with green and she carries with her a strange rod of sinuous silver, set with a emerald gemstone.

Ships:

The Pearl of Red Duchess

The largest Galleon of the Galacian Royal Merchant Guild. Manned by over three hundred women, men, and deckhands. Her bow is proud and her sails wide. Though, this ominous journey just break her masts.

The Black Sister

A dark ship known only in ghost stories.

Places:

Gal

Capital of the Nation of Galacia.

Port Amandri

Farthest port to the West, still under the control of the Republic of Ordiatea.

Duka'unka'falla

A cursed island known only in fairytales to exist. It is told a hidden treasure called the Heart resides deep within her jungles. The only problem is, no human can sail there, for it is beyond the ways of mortal man to find.

PRIEVEIW FROM:

CHAINS OF A BROKEN GOD
BOOK TWO OF THE LAST SON OF THE FEROMAGE SAGA

Icy wind stripped away the tears that coursed down Iaenora's face. She was alive - her vision blurred, and her consciousness waned, but she was alive.

Images flashed through her mind - memories long forgotten - some her own, others, the Vessel's. Iaenora struggled to maintain her grip on the mind. The bond was strong, but the body was dying. Without it, there was little hope of stopping what was to come.

Ahead, far in the distance, atop a green hill, rose a building of splendor and magnitude that harkened back to the before days. However, it was not the building's spires that drew Iaenora, but what lay beneath, dormant, asleep. A well of power, a great fissure in the earth leading down to a deeping pool of Aetora's Light. She had seen this pool when she touched the mind of that old priest. She had felt the familiar essence upon him, he had known Her power, intimately.

The edges of Iaenora's vision began to darken, all light narrowing to a singular pinprick of pulsating sapphire. The temple's ceiling gave way before her, she barely felt the pain as her body struck the stone. The floor cracked when Iaenora landed, dust and debris showering around her.

Forms moved about her. She could see them twice over - Their physical manifestations in white cloth and breastplates, their face's wrapped, and their Aethereal forms as shadows of misty white light that seemed to trail behind them. These moved swiftly as if they had no fear of death. They held long polearms and uttered not a sound.

Iaenora burst forward, tendrils of sapphire light leaking from her body. She had to get to the Source. She was fading. It felt like her soul was being torn into pieces with every motion. Iaenora wanted to howl in pain, but she did not. She could not. Every bit of focus, every ounce of being was pointed towards that fissure and to the Everlight that flowed beneath the surface of the earth.

Something hard struck her side, piercing flesh. Flesh was of little consequence right now. But the agony was undeniable. This form, this human s Iaenora had bonded with was of lesser matter. It did not act like her own body had before that horrid night, where her sisters failed, and the heavens wept.

No. this body was fragile, weak, and worst of all, mortal. If she could only get to the Light, she could mend this body; make it new, better.

Another halberd sank into her flesh, taking her in the back and driving her to the floor. She let out a gasp of pain, sapphire light misting from her mouth as she cried. These were not her enemies. She had seen them, in that priest's mind. They were only trying to protect this sacred place.

Iaenora raised a hand and forced out a gust of wind, not enough to kill, but enough to send these assailants flying backward. The motion weakened her to near immobility. Using her hands, she pulled herself across the floor. A door stood between her and a chamber where the Essence was near. She could smell it, an electric scent mixed with a sharp tinge of freshness. Her body craved the Light - needed it more than anything else.

With a final push, Iaenora burst the door from its hinges. Metal groaned under the strain of the blast, then gave way. Cogs and chains clacked and clanged as the apertures sealing the room failed. Aluth, those guards, that was their title, rose from the ground and began to pursue her. Iaenora, taking in a final breath of air, thrust herself forwards, into a room she had seen before - not in her own mind, but that of the priest's - past the rows of benches and against the crevasse in the floor.

Blue light shone from beneath the vents. Iaenora grasped the grates as Aluth stormed the room. She screamed in agony, yanking the metal from the stone. Her cry reverberated through the chamber, causing the Aluth to stop and stare in wonder. Giving a final look at the guards, Iaenora tipped over sideways and plummeted into the depths, consciousness fleeting from before her very eyes as she fell into nothingness - into Light eternal.